DANGER'S HALO

A HOLLY DANGER NOVEL:
BOOK ONE

AMANDA CARLSON

OTHER BOOKS BY AMANDA CARLSON

Jessica McClain Series:
Urban Fantasy
BLOODED
FULL BLOODED
HOT BLOODED
COLD BLOODED
RED BLOODED
PURE BLOODED
BLUE BLOODED

Sin City Collectors:
Paranormal Romance
ACES WILD
ANTE UP
ALL IN

Phoebe Meadows:
Contemporary Fantasy
STRUCK
FREED
EXILED

Holly Danger:
Futuristic Dystopian
DANGER'S HALO
DANGER'S VICE
DANGER'S RACE
DANGER'S CURE
DANGER'S HUNT
DANGER'S FATE

For Billy, the tech master

Chapter 1

"Nobody survives that jump, kid." Judging by the boy's ragged clothing, he'd been living on the streets for a while. He couldn't have been more than about ten. "It's a lie. They tell you that so they can steal from you once they discover your dead, mangled body on the rocks below."

I kicked the door of my dronecraft shut with the tip of a titanium-toed boot. The vehicle rocked, but held steady. I ignored the grating whir coming from the motor as I made my way over to where the urchin stood, his toes already too close to the edge. I kept the craft running to err on the side of safety. We were out pretty far, and it was getting close to dark. Save for the water rushing in the gorge sixty meters below, the desolate landscape was like everything around here: cold, dreary, dirty, and mostly dead.

I flipped the visor on my helmet down to keep the slanting rain out of my eyes. Swirling gray clouds were a near-constant sight and provided ongoing precipitation on most days. The only good thing about the moisture was it kept the iron dust down to a minimum, making air masks voluntary, except for the handful of days when the drizzle cleared, which numbered fewer than the fingers on one hand.

The kid had decided to ignore me. Couldn't really blame him.

Crisp wind abraded my cheeks, the only skin exposed to the elements, the temperature always on the verge of too damn cold. My boots crunched over the ground, rocks skittering and bouncing in and out of dark, red-tinted puddles as I made my way toward him. I was dressed in head-to-toe leather. The usual: pants, jacket, vest, gloves.

Well, I wasn't *actually* wearing animal hide, since all the livestock and most of the wild animals had been extinct for years, but we still called it that. Old habits. The synthetic texture was *leatherlike,* so the name had endured. As had many others. The consensus was that it was too hard to find new names for stuff, and no one really gave a shit what you called it anyway.

I was almost to him when he finally decided to speak. "They…they said if I survived I could go live on the Flotilla." His voice wavered, reeking of fatigue, but stubbornly holding on to a single kernel of hope—that leaving this wretched place for something better was possible. It wasn't.

"Whoever told you that was lying." I tried to make my voice sound less like I wanted to throat-punch someone, since I was dealing with a child, but I had one dial, and it was always set to the same channel. That's what years in this city did to you. It set your dial. I stuffed my gloved hands into my pockets. "Besides, how do you know that place even exists?"

The Flotilla was mostly a myth for those of us who'd been born after the mass exodus. That fateful day when the wealthy took their vast resources and launched The Water Initiative, which, according to the records left behind, consisted of a massive fleet of boats and barges stuffed with most of the city's critical supplies. The entire brigade had sailed out of the harbor without so much as a backward glance, flipping the city a gigantic finger in its wake.

I'd heard the same rumors this kid had growing up—that the water city had flourished, was clean and chock full of food, commerce, and fresh, breathable air.

Everything we lacked here.

Assholes.

"The Flotilla exists," the urchin insisted. "I heard from a runner, who heard from a peddler, who heard from a guard, that the Flotilla is running out of supplies and they need hard workers to rebuild after a great storm. I'm a hard worker." He thumped his chest, his face grimy and smeared with dirt.

On second thought, he was probably more like eight than ten.

I'd recently heard similar tales, and so had my crew, but unlike the kid, we'd written it off as gossip, like every other piece of information about that place. It ranked up there with other news I'd heard recently, like: Rain was in the forecast for this week, or protein cakes were delicious. They weren't.

"I'm sure there's no harder worker." I peered over the edge. The drop would kill him instantly. Hell, it would kill anyone. I couldn't blame him for believing the stories, however. There were always stories. And, honestly, who wouldn't want to trade their shitty lives to be transported to a watery haven with fresh, breathable air and food that didn't crumble down your chin every time you ate it? Most of us would take the same running leap off a cliff if that were the case.

"They said it was about time someone survived," he said. "I'd even get a parade thrown in my honor."

"A parade?" Was this kid serious? "Honestly, have you ever glimpsed a parade in this town?"

"I've seen pictures," he boasted. "In the zoom tunnels. There's a bunch of stuff on the walls down there. The photos are torn and faded, but they exist. They had lots of colorful animals filled with air, and people were smiling." His voice held hope. Poor bastard.

"Pictures you find in dank undergrounds don't represent our world today. You should know better than to listen to street gossip."

He glared at me out of the corner of a soot-streaked eye, not appearing even a little bit convinced. He wanted to believe, and I was the big bad bitch who was going to stomp all over his dreams. "Listen, being gullible will get you killed quicker than a laser straight through the eye. Now, let's get out of here. I've got important things to do today, like putting my feet up after my long journey out here." He didn't respond. "Today is not your day to die, kid. I promise. Get in my craft, and I'll haul your skinny ass back to the city." I gestured with my thumb toward my ride. A standard-issue A1 military dronecraft. "I call her Lucy, Luce for short."

"That thing is a wreck." He peered around me, scoffing. "I'm surprised it still runs."

I arched an eyebrow at the kid, who had now decided he had some backbone. "I'll have you know that this was my grandfather's. He served in the militia until 2141. He handed it down to me, name and all, and I've kept her running ever since."

"It looks like your grandpa's. A1 is ancient. The new ones are W6's. That's almost the entire alphabet."

I sighed. *New* was a relative term around here. They'd stopped making crafts thirty years ago, after the Flotilla left with all the remaining resources. "Honestly, kid, if you want to live, get in the craft." I swept a hand in front of me. "Or be my guest and shatter yourself on the rocks below. I get paid either way." His jaw stuck out stubbornly and his skinny arms were locked in front of him. He was going to be a tough sell. "You might as well give me your tag." I held out my palm. "At least I can give it to your next of kin once you perish in spectacular fashion. I promise not to describe to them how your body looked splattered all over the rocks, and I usually keep my word." I always kept my word.

"I don't have a tag."

"What do you mean?" Everyone had a tag. They were government-issued IDs and were the *only* way to get sustenance and supplies on a regular basis. The food rations were crappy and came in the form of dry, crumbly protein blocks, but they kept us from gnawing our arms off or killing our irritating neighbors to stay alive. Most of the 3-D bio-printers were inactive, and those that still ran worked at limited capacity, based on their size and the fact we had few ingredients to fill them.

"I gave it away."

"Seriously?" I didn't even give a crap about this child, but I was floored. "Hold out your wrist." He turned it over, and sure enough, there was a divot where the tag should've been. His skin was puckered and pink. "It can take up to a year to get new ones," I warned. Tags were inserted at birth. They were a centimeter wide and less than a millimeter thick. They contained a frequency and symbol combination that was uniquely your own. As you grew, your flesh secured them. No one remembered how it felt to have them inserted, so no one complained. "Why'd you go and do a stupid thing like that?"

"Why do you care?" he shot back, flashing me a look of disdain that was praiseworthy—if I was in the mood to give out compliments, which I wasn't.

"Who said I do? But that was dumb. If you live on the streets, you should know better."

"I don't."

"Don't what?"

"Live on the streets. Well, I do now, since I ran away." He stuck out his chin. "But I didn't used to."

"Where was home?" I crossed my arms, which was an accomplishment in my vest. It was fashioned from carbon fiber and was tase resistant, but not laser impenetrable—because there was nothing on the battered face of this Earth that would stop a concentrated blast of electromagnetic radiation. It was bulky and thick because my pockets were always stuffed with crap that could potentially save my life. But I managed to hook my wrists and get them comfortably wedged between my elbows.

"Port Station."

"Why'd you run?"

"Because I hated it there."

"Did the city treat you any better?" Port Station was a heavily guarded community just outside city limits. "Because it doesn't look like it to me."

He glanced down, likely battling back tears. I didn't blame him. Crying here was the norm. Emotions had a way of eventually bubbling out. If not from the eyes, from the fists. "Everywhere is horrible." He kicked a stone. It arced over the side, dropping out of sight into the rushing water below.

"I can't argue with you there." Joy had been known to happen on occasion, but you had to search for it. And most of the time you were too tired to go looking.

"I want to live on the water or nowhere." He shuffled a titch closer to the edge. "I'm not scared to die."

I dropped my arms, suddenly wary of watching this

kid plunge to his death. Yet another casualty of this city. "Don't do it." I'd felt like him a dozen million times. "Come back with me and give life another try. I know people. We can try to find a boat captain. Maybe they'll take you on as a steward, or whatever hard workers on ships are called." It was a lie, but worth telling if the kid didn't jump. There were no boat captains, because there were no boats.

He shook his head slowly. "No."

I tried another tactic. "Do you know who I am?"

He peered at me sideways. "Why would I?"

"I take it you haven't been out of Port Station long, because I'm pretty famous. That's why I'm here. Someone paid me real coin to bring you back, and I used my honest-to-goodness tracking skills to find you." Leaving out that I'd known exactly where he'd be from the note I'd found stuffed in my slot. Lies were important when told well. "I'm that good."

"You tracked me in that rattling junk heap?"

I suppressed a smile. "It's not about the craft, it's about the lady who wields it." When he didn't take the bait, I pressed an index finger solidly into my chest. "Me. I'm talking about me. I'm the best salvager out there. I can find just about anything if given enough time, including runaways who give their tags away like dummies."

"What's your name, then?"

Since I had no way to amp up the reveal, I settled on a dramatic pause. When a sufficient amount of time passed, I answered, "Holly Danger."

He shrugged. "So what?"

"Come on, you've heard of me. Admit it."

"Yeah."

Okay, my status was non-impressive. Good to know. "I just heard about a new initiative they're starting. They're talking about shuttling people down South. There's a rumor the sun is trying to break through there. The land is supposed to become habitable in a few years."

"They're always coming up with initiatives. They never work."

"The Flotilla worked, or you wouldn't be standing here willing to end your life for it."

He shrugged his twiggy shoulders. Nothing but bones popping against the thin fabric. The kid wanted to check out. Even if I could grab him before he flung himself over, and managed to haul him into Luce and back to the city, he'd likely dive out a megascraper window the first chance he got. Most of the scrapers didn't have glass anymore, which made plunging to your death incredibly easy. It was a popular way to go.

"Death is final," I cautioned. "There's no coming back, no second chances."

"I don't care. I don't want to come back."

"Do you have family? Next of kin in Port Station?"

"No," he answered dismally. "My mom died of the plague last year, and I never knew my dad. My sustainer family was going to sell me into slavery, so I ran."

The story unfolded.

Sickness was rampant everywhere. If you didn't have enough seniority or an effective way to bribe yourself an inoculation, which were heavily rationed, you were done for. We called everything "the plague," because no one knew what they had. Most viruses were hybrids with genetically modified components. Before the dark days, people enjoyed perfect health. Sickness had been completely wiped out. Nanobiotechnology, where a single manufactured cell was programmed to obliterate an invader cell, had been highly effective. But after the world my ancestors knew ended, disease eventually crept back in, and cures and inoculations were scarce.

"You must have someone," I coaxed. "They gave me coin to recover you, remember?"

"I bet it was Tandor," he replied glumly.

"Who's Tandor?"

There were very few names in this town I didn't recognize. It was my job to know who was who, and I took it seriously. I was a salvager and all-around procurer of things. It provided a living above and beyond table scraps and protein blocks. I had spaces filled with goods to sell scattered all over the city that no one knew anything about. I planned to keep it that way.

To be fair, though, the job of tracking down this kid had come in the form of an anonymous note and a bunch of coin dumped directly into one of my contact slots—which were hard to find. You had to know people. And I didn't make it a habit to turn down actual, physical currency, no matter what the job was.

Coin was still traded, and collectors held an affinity for it. A good collector would trade you a week's worth of protein or slurry for a single coin. Collectors were another name for the hopeful souls who were banking their entire existence on the return of the elite, when, they believed, physical currency would be reinstated.

Coin kept me in business.

The kid ran a grimy shirtsleeve under his nose. "Tandor's new in town. He's…a bad man."

My interest level jumped to inquisitively piqued. "You don't say." I tried not to sound surprised that this urchin knew something I didn't. I'd heard rumors that there were new outskirts in town, but the info had been hush-hush and low to the ground. Fairly typical when the topic revolved around child slavery, which I took seriously—not just because it was repugnant and vile, but because I had a personal stake.

At any one time, the city was overrun with orphans, and snatching them was nothing new. The street kids had little means to fight back and could be used for all kinds of purposes, most of them horrific, including experimentation. There were very few options for scientific testing, so when orphans "volunteered" for the good of society, who was going to say no?

The moral code in this city bordered on nonexistent. The only code anyone took seriously was survival.

These kinds of crime rings were usually run by outskirts, strangers who rolled into town, armed and dangerous, flouting our laws and rules to further their own agenda. Or those who'd already been kicked out of town for whatever reason and had slunk back in, which meant death if they were caught. The government didn't give second chances. It barely gave firsts. Its favorite method of punishing someone for a high crime was an over-the-head acid dump. The lucky assholes got banishment.

The outskirts came, took what they wanted, wreaked havoc, and moved on. Most of the time. Occasionally, they stayed. Or tried to stay. That's when we got in the way.

"You don't know who he is, do you?" The kid was downright gleeful at my ignorance, actually cracking a real smile. His teeth were pretty clean, which wasn't the norm. You had to work at it.

I took a step closer, coming up with something on the spot. "Listen, I have a proposition for you. You'd be an idiot to turn it down. I'm not known for sharing anything with anyone, so this would be a first for me."

He looked me straight in the eyes. "I'm no idiot."

Yes, kid, that was becoming abundantly clear.

Chapter 2

"Come with me, tell me all you know about this Tandor, and I'll be your sustainer for one year." I held up a single finger, scrunching it up and down. Just so he didn't get any ideas that it would be a day longer than that specified timeframe.

Right after the words left my mouth, I glanced down at the rushing water below and contemplated jumping. Had I actually made that proposition *out loud?* I'd never offered to be anyone's sustainer in my entire life, which meant the dirty air I'd been inhaling since exiting the womb was officially affecting my brain—that, or the thing in my chest was searching for some much-needed exercise. I mean, the kid had moxie, but I hadn't stretched those muscles since my mother died nineteen years ago. After she left this Earth, my heartstrings had all but atrophied. Which, honestly, I was fine with. Foul air was likely to blame. I probably had so many iron particles built up in my brain, my synapses were misfiring.

Being a sustainer basically meant I agreed to make sure this kid had food, adequate clothing, and a place to lay his head every night that was free from the constant cold, shitty drizzle that fell from our sunless sky. One usually did it out of the kindness of his or her heart—or apparently, if the air messed with her mind.

"*You* want to sustainer me?" His voice sounded incredulous, which pretty much mirrored how I felt. "Shut up. You're lying."

"I'm not." I refused to retract my offer, even though my internal struggle was making me mildly queasy. What was I going to do with a goddamn *kid*? "I need information, and you have it." That was valid enough. "Plus, I could use your small hands and body to weasel into places I can't reach. I have my eye on a few quality items, but I'm having trouble accessing them. If you're lucky, I can train you to be a kickass salvager, but only if you pay close attention. I don't baby anyone, so it's on you to keep up."

He looked unsure, but took a minute step back. It was a start. "They'll kill me if they find me," he said. "Especially if they see me with you."

I shrugged. "I'll tell them you're dead. You jumped before I got here. End of story."

"They'll come check, and they won't see a body," he pointed out.

"Sometimes people hit the rocks and roll into the water."

"Not without leaving any blood."

He was right. I turned and strode purposefully back to Luce, yanking open the flat storage compartment in the back. Sliding a large box forward, I searched until I found the vial I was looking for, and slammed everything shut. Then I walked to the passenger door, lofted it, and grabbed a jug. I made it back to the side of the gorge in less than two minutes, where the kid had been standing watching me. I set the jug on the ground, poured the contents of the vial into it, and shook.

"What are you doing?"

"Making it look like you died a bloody, painful death." I popped the top off and emptied the contents over the side. We both watched as red, sloppy goop splattered all over the rocks below.

"That's pretty gruesome."

"Do I detect a note of awe in your voice?"

"Possibly." The corner of his mouth went up in a half smile. Once the dirt and grime disappeared, he might look decent. "But I haven't agreed to go with you yet."

"Oh, you will," I said confidently as I headed back to the craft, tossing the jug inside, leaving the door open. I walked around to the control side and got in.

I had to wait a total of thirty-seven seconds before the urchin climbed in.

The kid wanted to live after all.

"Ew, it stinks in here," he said as he reached up to bring the door down, making a show of covering his nose with his whole hand once he settled into the seat.

"Get used to it. I have a lot of stuff in here. Stuff I need. Some of it smells." I took off, gunning the propulsion, half trying to impress the kid, half trying to get the hell out of here, because the red light on my dash had started to blink. Another craft was in close proximity. "Hit the floor," I instructed. "We've got company, and if I can't lose them, things are going to get tricky fast."

"The space is too tight."

"Make it work, kid. That's your new motto. Life is hard. Make it work." I jammed the lever in my left hand toward the windshield, careening Luce forward, gaining speed. My right hand worked the props, increasing altitude.

"How'd you get the name Holly Danger, anyway?" he asked as he scrunched down in an effort to fit into a space intended for adult-sized feet. I reached a hand into the back and dragged out an old blanket, tossing it over him. "Gross! This reeks like vomit!"

I jerked Luce to the right as the red light began to flicker without ceasing. We were on an old forest path that had been cleared of trees once upon a time but now contained low, dead brush, which was ideal for keeping concealed below the tree line.

Another quick few turns and I whipped Luce behind a stand of dead pines, slowing her props, dipping her close to the ground. These trees were as decent cover as any, due to their many branches, even if they were devoid of most of their needles.

I fixated on the blinking light, watching as the

pulses began to spread out. When I was confident that the other craft had turned in the opposite direction, I answered the kid's question. "My real name is Hollywood California." We were going to be here for a bit, so I lifted a boot up and rested it on the console between the seats. The kid wasn't kidding, space was tight, and I had long legs. "You weren't the only one who found old pictures in tunnels and got grand ideas. My mother discovered a bunch of things called postcards when she was pregnant with me and took a special liking to one that had a tree with a long, skinny trunk and broad leaves like fan blades, an ocean that was aqua instead of putrid green, and a huge ball of sunshine sparkling in the corner. It was captioned *Hollywood, California.*" I still had it tucked away. One of my meager possessions worth saving. "My mom told me that postcard was the most beautiful thing she'd ever laid eyes on. When she gave birth to me, she said it was time the two beauties in her life met. So, I was thusly named."

"What about the Danger part?" He coughed, wiggling his nose out from under the blanket—which was really just a large piece of raggedy cloth that had been in my craft for too many years to count. It had a variety of substances on it I couldn't name. It was totally gross.

The blinking on the dash switched to yellow. That was a good sign. The other craft was now at least three kilometers away. We'd be in the clear soon.

"As a kid, I got into everything. My mom constantly yelled, 'Holly, don't touch that, it's dangerous.' 'Holly, don't do that, it's dangerous.' She eventually shortened it to 'Holly, danger!' and it stuck. Not exactly edge-of-your-seat stuff." Instead of the light switching to solid green, like it should have, it began to flicker yellow again, the time between blinks shrinking rapidly. Then it went red. Fuck. Not in the clear. "Stay low," I murmured, repositioning my leg near the converter, readying myself for a quick exit. "Another craft is entering the area. They won't be able to pinpoint us exactly, but if they have any sophisticated tech, they know we're here somewhere. We might have to hide out here until blackout just to be safe."

"Blackout?" He rubbed his eyes, which had begun to water in earnest. "That means we won't make it back into the city before dark."

I detected fear in his voice for the first time. "What's your name?"

"Robert, but everyone calls me Daze."

"Daze, I'm going to give you the benefit of the doubt here, because you don't know me. But nothing keeps me out of *my* city, blackout or not. I have connections, know every back road and every crack in the mortar from here past Port Station. Luce may look old, but she's retrofitted with the most up-to-date tech available." Which wasn't saying much, but it was a step up from what regular folks had access to. "Right now, she's scattering the other craft's radar, making it seem we're much farther away than we actually are. From now on, there's no doubting me. Keep it up and it'll be the quickest way to get you kicked out of my life."

"But you promised to sustainer me for a year." He sniffed three times, ending on a sneeze.

"Yeah, I did. But I forgot to mention that our new arrangement is dependent on how symbiotic our relationship becomes. It's going to go like this: You trust me unconditionally, give me information when I ask, and I keep you alive. We clear?"

"Clear."

The red light on the dash solidified.

Luce was painted a dull gray, to blend in, for this very reason. The craft had actually been painted every color of the rainbow at one point or another, but dead gray matched the bleak landscape the best. "Stay down," I ordered Daze. "They're on top of us. And, by the way, why are they tracking you so hard?" I raised an eyebrow toward the scrunched-up face peeking out at me. "It seems like a lot of effort for a runaway." Actually, come to think of it, I'd never been paid to find a street kid before. Nobody, except for a handful of folks, with actual working, beating hearts, cared about lost kids.

"I did something I wasn't supposed to." His voice was barely above a whisper.

"Is that so?"

"Yes." He pushed the blanket a few centimeters away from his face and gulped in a few big breaths. "I snuck into Tandor's office when he was out on a run and stole something important."

"Now why would you go and do a thing like that?" This kid had run away from Port Station, fallen into something over his head, and now he was caught in the middle of a brewing shitstorm. Those kinds of storms circled this city on a regular basis, and once you were sucked in, it was hard to come out the other side unscathed.

"I was trying to save my friend."

"Noble." In front of us, through the trees, I spotted what appeared to be a Q7 dronecraft creeping forward. It was matte black and slightly bigger than Luce. The Q's had several features that had made them marketable back in the day. The 7's, in particular, were a favorite, as they had bigger props, which provided a faster ride. Those same features were changed in the 8's, as the larger props in the 7's made the crafts too heavy and therefore unstable. There'd been a hell of a lot of crashes. Whoever chose a Q7 was in it for speed and had to be a damn good pilot.

The only reason the driver wasn't checking the brush around them was that Luce's radar expander was making them think she was up the road a good half kilometer.

Once they passed, I pulled back hard, shooting Luce in reverse.

I maneuvered her through the trees, using my eyes and skills, not autopilot, which had become a nonexistent feature once the satellites had been knocked out of the sky by all the shit floating around in the atmosphere.

"I was too late to save my friend." The ride began to get wavy, and the kid had to grip the seat in front of him to stay put, the blanket tumbling back, the look of relief on his face endearing.

"Sorry to hear that." My arm was braced across the back of his seat, neck craned, eyes pinned out the back windshield, occasionally darting a glance forward. Dodging obstacles in reverse was one of my favorite pastimes. I could do it in my sleep.

"She was my only friend. But I got Tandor back." A shit-eating grin emerged. "I took something, and he wants it back bad."

Daze was ready to talk.

"What'd you steal, kid?"

Chapter 3

I nearly crashed the back end of Luce into a thicket of trees, this time a stand of old oaks with peeling, gray bark. All of them were dead, their upper branches gnarled and black. They could be on their way to petrified, it was hard to know.

"What did you just say?" I asked as I brought the craft to a jerky stop, keeping her idling.

Daze was on his knees, forehead braced against the bottom of the seat he'd been forced to hang on to for dear life to stop from tumbling around.

I could dodge anything, but I never said it would be a smooth ride.

Instead of telling me, the kid lifted his head and dug in his pocket, drawing out something that looked remarkably like a quantum drive. It was no bigger than a two-centimeter square, coated in nano-carbon with a row of barely there input holes running along one end. "I took this." He set the curious object in my outstretched palm.

I brought it in for a closer look.

"I've only seen one of these in my entire life." I refrained from gaping, because that would've been strange and alarming for the kid. "This technology isn't supposed to exist anymore. This little chip"—I held it between my thumb and forefinger—"can hold every word, number, or piece of data in existence before the meteor hit. And the only way to read it is on something called a pico." A superfast computer that hadn't been around since the elite left town. Picos did everything a computer did, but reading, formatting, and transferring data to quantum drives was their specialty.

Crafters had tried to restart the technology, creating new superfast computers from spare parts, but they always failed because of the microscopic connections needed to engage with this finicky quantum drive.

I couldn't believe I had one resting in my hand.

Daze crawled onto the seat, looking pale from our exciting adventure. "Your flying stinks, by the way." He blew out his cheeks and held his stomach, looking like he was trying hard not to lose his breakfast. That was, if he'd eaten at all. By the look of his painfully thin shoulders, the answer was no. "Tandor has a pico. It works, I saw it."

"My flying is awesome, by the way, and it just saved your little, scrawny hide, so a thank-you is in order. And if Tandor has a pico, our world just got more complicated." I glanced at the light on the dash. It'd gone solid green sometime during my retreat. I flipped a lever, sending a signal to the other craft, making them think a third vessel had entered the area on the other side of the gorge, just to further mess with things. Just the way I liked it.

I sat back, propping my boot back on the console, sending a silent but grateful message to Bender for his mad skills when it came to installing tech in my craft. He was the best in the business.

"Thanks," Daze muttered.

"You're welcome. And, honestly, if you knew how hard it is to maneuver a craft backward, constant praise would be running from your mouth." I arched an eyebrow at him as I flipped the drive over in my hand. "We're going to hang out here for a while, and once I deem it clear, we'll make our way back into the city. We should be there by blackout, but no guarantees. And no second-guessing allowed," I warned as I popped open a small compartment underneath the steering levers. "If it's okay with you, I'm going to put this in here for safekeeping. I know it's yours, and I'm not confiscating it, but if Tandor wants it that bad, we have to secure it. For now, that means here." I snapped the door shut. "Nobody knows how to open this hiding spot but me, and now you, if you were paying attention. Luce has lots of hidey holes. They've come in handy over the years." I stroked her dash affectionately, giving her a few taps for luck. "She's one of a kind."

"Tandor is going to kill me for taking that," Daze said despondently, his gaze firmly directed out the window. "I don't care what you do with it. I never want to see it again."

I crossed my arms, one eye on the green light, one on the dejected kid with his bottom lip out. "If you knew it would get you killed, why'd you take it?" I asked, even though I knew the answer.

In this town, friends were few and far between. If Daze thought he was helping his buddy, he would've done anything. I lived in that space. I knew it well.

"I overheard them talking one night," he started. "Tandor was bragging to his partner about how he got his hands on this high-tech computer and how nobody would ever be able to decipher the information. He said he put it all in there—names, dates, and everything—and if he was caught, he'd just trash it."

"But you managed to sleuth it out," I said. "And why is that? From what I know—and full confession here, my knowledge is limited because superfast computers are rare and complicated—that quantum drive had to have been tucked into a slot inside the pico, hidden from view." I didn't even know where, because even though I'd seen a single drive before, I'd never laid eyes on a pico. "How'd you know how to get to it?"

Daze plucked at a frayed edge of the dirty blanket that was stuffed mostly at his feet. "Because my mom had one, and I used to play around on it."

My knee jerked, hitting the dash with a painful thump. "*What?*" I reached up and yanked off my helmet, mopping the hair away from my face with splayed fingers. It was tangled and sweaty from being under an unbreathable shield all day, like usual. I tossed my helmet in the back. Daze's eyes widened as he took me in without coverage for the first time. "You just had a pico lying around your place? Care to explain why you had a supercomputer—something the government may or may not even have—collecting dust around your residence?"

"Um." His eyes were locked on me, his mouth slightly ajar.

"What? Snap out of it. Yes, I'm female. We've already met."

"I just…I've never seen someone like you before," he mumbled, his fists wadding up the stanky blanket. Then, realizing what he was doing, he shoved it off his legs with a huff. "Ew. You need to burn that thing."

"I'll get right on it. Now answer my question. Why did you have a pico? And do you still have it?" He tried to meet my eyes, but he blushed and glanced away. I sighed. "How old are you, Daze?"

"Twelve."

"*Twelve?*" I couldn't insult him by shouting that he looked like an eight-year-old. "I thought you were—"

"Younger. I know. I'm small for my age." He stuck his chin out in a move I was going to christen The Daze. "But it's about what's up here and the boy who wields it." He tapped his temple.

"Nice." I grinned. "We're going to get along just fine." I readjusted myself, rubbed my knee, and launched Luce into action—this time forward instead of in reverse. "While I pick my way out of here, in between acres of dead, twisted trees, you're going to explain to me exactly how and why you had access to a pico."

"On one condition," he countered.

Now there were conditions? "And what's that?"

"We crack a window in here. It stinks like rotten slurry."

"Fine, kid," I said. "Be my guest. But you better not stop talking the entire way back. I'm expecting nonstop diarrhea of the mouth. Every single detail uttered, nothing left unsaid."

Daze cracked a small triangular window in front as I took off. I was planning to take the long way back.

This kid needed time to spill.

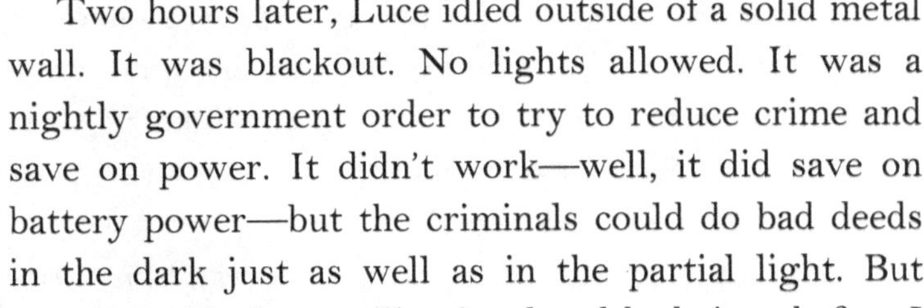

Two hours later, Luce idled outside of a solid metal wall. It was blackout. No lights allowed. It was a nightly government order to try to reduce crime and save on power. It didn't work—well, it did save on battery power—but the criminals could do bad deeds in the dark just as well as in the partial light. But somehow, blackout still existed and had since before I was born.

Daze leaned forward, squinting through the windshield. "I thought you said you knew where you were going? You even bragged about it. That's a building, and all the entrances into the city are blocked. If we stay here much longer, UACs will find us."

Unmanned aerial crafts were a popular way for the government to keep eyes on its citizens. They claimed the small drones were for our protection, but because of the iron-laced air, UACs weren't able to send live feed without massive interruptions. So all the drones could do was record reputed "bad" behavior, then zip back to their holding docks like the automated tattletales they were. By the time the government uploaded the files, most anyone with a brain was long gone.

The only problem was that the compromising footage went into a "file," and if you were ever unlucky enough to get arrested, they could use it against you.

"I wasn't bragging," I said. "It's called swagger. All the cool kids have it." I twisted the controls, throwing my shoulder into it, and spun Luce around to angle her backside at a specific location on the wall. The move had been effortless, but I hadn't warned Daze, who'd toppled into my lap during my expert steering maneuver. "You may want to use the shoulder straps next time." I gave him a snarky grin. "They're there for a reason and come in handy when you're in the company of an *excellent* pilot."

Daze gathered himself up quickly, scrambling back into his seat, his skinny arms tugging their way through the shoulder harness, buckling it with a loud clack. He gave me a side-eye. "You could've warned me."

"Lesson number two." I held up two fingers as I reached over and tapped a black button on the dash. "Everything I do is on-the-job training. If your brain is not awesome enough to figure it out, not my fault. You almost lost your cookies when I flew Luce in reverse. That should've been warning enough." Behind us, a small seam in the facade began to grow, quickly becoming a gaping hole. "I mean, it's not like you couldn't *see* the shoulder harness. It's always been there. Kind of like a welcome gift reaching out, aching to protect you, to feel the warmth of your body heating up its straps. It's not there for decoration, no matter how pretty it seems. In fact, it's—"

"You can stop now. I get it," he muttered as he glanced out the back window. "Where are we?"

"I call this 'almost home.'" The wall now had a craft-size hole. A single light flashed, and I began to back her up.

Once inside, the wall in front of us silently shuttered. It didn't make a peep. It was virtually impervious to any assault, except a very high-powered laser, because, well, it was graphene—3-D printed graphite, composed in a multilayered honeycomb matrix, making it super tough and durable. Graphene was still produced in limited amounts, regulated by the government. Most of ours had come from salvaging. Like most of my stuff.

I waited until the seam had fully engaged before I popped Luce's door and got out. Daze began to follow. "Stay inside," I said, reaching into my vest to produce a high-powered light no bigger than the tip of my finger. "I have to punch in some codes. Then we move."

I made my way over to a panel on the wall, my light

producing a big, bright arc in front of me. To the naked eye, the box resembled an old electrical panel, complete with wires spilling out. The wires had been left behind from when these buildings had been massively upgraded before the dark days, decades ago.

In reality, the panel held a security board known to only a select few.

That few included me, Bender, Claire, Lockland, and Darby. My crew. The only folks I trusted with my life in this city. It'd taken a hell of a long time for me to widen my network of trust beyond Bender and Claire, but eventually I had, and the five of us each brought a different skill to the table. That's why it worked.

It was symbiotic.

Working together kept us sane and out of the hands of the government. Most of the time. That was the only way to survive in this city. Staying alive was the primary goal. The secondary goal was to try to make our lives a little more comfortable—*comfort* being a relative term when most of the things relating to that word had been destroyed a long time ago.

Careful to touch only the black wires, not the red, I located a keypad and punched in the code. I waited not too patiently for the light to come on. After a few seconds, it did. It was orange.

Orange meant check-in.

I walked back to Luce and got in, bringing the door down out of habit. I opened up the console and dug around for a small tech phone. As far as communication went, low frequency radio was basically all we had. Not much else could penetrate the iron dust. It'd been a miracle that longwave technology had lingered as long as it had in the high frequency, shortwave world that had flourished in its place. Even more amazing was that we'd been able to modify it. Sixty-some years after the meteor took out life as my ancestors had known it, we hadn't achieved much, but we did have low frequency. Without it, life would be so much more irritating.

"Is that a tech phone?" Daze's eyes had widened. "Cool. I've never seen one, only heard about them."

I checked the knob to make sure it was set on channel ten, one of our obscure bandwidths that no one else used. Even though direct communication was ours, anybody with access to a radio receiver, which were quite a few, since it was a source of entertainment around here, could listen in. So we were careful to speak in code.

I depressed the button and spoke clearly into the speaker. "Johnny, it's Ella. My sewage separator is backed up again. Can you come help me fix it?"

Static came across the line, followed by, "No can do." Bender's voice held an edge, and I leaned forward. "I'm staying put tonight. See if Jerry's available."

"Okay, thanks." I flicked my finger off the button and stuffed the phone into a vest pocket. Then I reached back for my helmet and slid it on. "I thought we could fly out, but we're going to walk. I have another hard hat in the back, but I can't guarantee it's not going to stink. Want it or not?" Strolling around the city without protective headgear was taking your life in your own hands. A helmet not only deflected the rain and provided a built-in infrared visor, but it protected your skull from falling debris that tumbled down from the scrapers frequently enough to give you brain damage if you weren't careful. The helmets themselves were extremely thin and lightweight, made from molded micro-Kevlar. The visor was essential. Without night vision, it would be difficult to get around during blackout or anytime at night, and sometimes during the day when the rain was heavy.

"I guess," Daze answered tentatively. "What did he mean, 'See if Jerry's available'?"

"That was code, kid. You have to be careful what you say over the open airwaves." I searched for a helmet that wasn't too beat-up. There wasn't much I didn't have in this craft. However, anything I had in the back would be way too big for Daze, but he'd make do. I found one and plunked it in his lap. "I asked if it was safe to fly home, he said no, that there are heavy patrols out tonight, so don't even think about it. Make it to the nearest safe house and settle in. Oh, and he said somebody's looking for me, so watch my back."

"He said all that?" Daze's face was incredulous.

I nodded. "That he did. Bender's a man of few words, but he makes every one of them count. I got the 'somebody's looking for you, so watch your back' from his tone. Every single thing matters when you're communicating across radio waves. Never forget. It's the difference between staying alive and being dead."

I punched Luce off. Her landing gear engaged, and she slowly sank to the ground with a little bounce at the end. Once she was settled on her rubber pads, I popped the door open and got out. Daze followed out the passenger side.

"Where are we going?" he asked, buzzing around the back, donning his way-too-big headgear.

"To the canals." I tried not to react to his expression, which was a straight-up mixture of shock and horror. My flashlight lit up the entire room as I made my way toward a door on the other side. Our visors were useless in here, because this space was devoid of all light. The beauty of infrared was it made use of any and all available light, allowing you to see in the dark—just not total blackness. For that, you needed a light. Like the one in my hand or the ones on my shoulders, conveniently attached to my vest.

Daze balked, trailing after me. "You can't be serious."

"Dead." The retina scanner on the wall had long been defunct, but Darby had rigged up a fingerprint reader. The door we were exiting was twenty-centimeters-thick titanium with several layers of graphene sandwiched in the middle. To get through without a thumbprint, you'd need a megawatt laser. It could be done, but who carried a megawatt around? Those things were as big as trash bins.

Daze was still sputtering. "But...but the canals are dangerous...and nobody but seekers live there. Not even outskirts."

"That's true, for the most part," I agreed as I settled my right thumb into the indentation. "The canals are a wild place, but if you know where you're going, they can be a safe haven. Because, see, if no bad guys are there, and you know how to avoid the seekers, that, my friend, equals safe." I wiggled my thumb. Nothing happened. My knee came up, jarring the box. Finally, a beep sounded, and a green light flickered over the doorknob.

I darted over to grasp the handle before the light extinguished. If I missed, I had to do the entire thing again. The techie's idea of hilarity. Darby thought it would be funny to force people to make the grab in under two seconds. It would've been even more amusing if the box actually worked regularly. I'd been stranded down here one time too many to see any humor in the situation.

The door swung freely.

I snapped off my light and stuffed it back in my pocket, flicking my visor down, waiting a few seconds for my eyes to adjust. "Follow me closely," I instructed. "If I hold my hand up, stop and stay absolutely quiet. Not one peep. We clear?"

"Clear." His voice was muffled. The helmet I'd given him had a full face mask built in. Wouldn't hurt to keep the kid covered for now. I had no idea how far this mysterious Tandor's reach went and who was searching for us.

"Also, no less than one meter separates us at all times. There are multiple ways to get where we're going, all dependent on who we encounter, and I'll be making decisions quickly." I wasn't used to worrying about someone else, much less a little kid with absolutely no body mass who had no idea how to defend himself and no weapons at his disposal.

With decided conviction, I cut off my inner brain before it eviscerated itself with slashing rebuttals about my stupid choice of offering myself up as a sustainer.

Why couldn't I have chosen a month instead of a year? That would've been so much easier. The kid probably would've taken it, too.

"Seekers. Is that who you mean?" Daze asked, his voice shooting for tough, but cracking around the edges. "Is that who we're going to encounter?"

"Not just the seekers," I said. "Remember, there are still outskirts crawling around out there."

"Outskirts know better than to lurk in the canals," Daze muttered, like he knew the inner workings of *my* city better than I did. "People talk, and outskirts listen. They aren't stupid or drugged up like the seekers."

He was right on that count. Seekers were "drugged up," as well as violent and unpredictable. After years of imbibing a powerful pleasure-seeking drug called Plush, their body chemistries had been permanently altered. Now their only focus was getting another fix, and they'd kill you without a moment's hesitation to achieve their goal.

Their behavior ranged between blissed-out after immediate ingestion to full-on rage-mode when they'd been without it for a day or two. They were extremely dangerous and uncontrollable, and they lived here, in the canals. It was the only place in the city the government left them alone. Very few people frequented the water maze, where the sea lashed against the crumbling buildings all day, every day. It wasn't a warm, fuzzy place to hang out, and getting around took effort. More than most wanted to put forth.

"Yeah," I replied blandly, "keep thinking like that and you'll be dead by morning. Just follow me and keep your head down."

"Won't be hard," he muttered. "It's the only way I can breathe without passing out. Does everything you own stink?"

Chapter 4

The view through my visor was granulated, shapes hazy and hard to differentiate, but it was better than nothing, and I was used to it. Even though the city was in blackout, the moonlight filtered through all the crap in the sky to provide tiny usable amounts of light. Most buildings contained enough holes to let the beams in. There wasn't anything standing in the entire world that hadn't been affected by the cataclysmic events that took place over sixty years ago. It was lucky we were even here at all.

We crept up two flights of stairs, Daze doing exactly what I asked, not letting a meter get between us. If I hadn't been so worried about him, I would have been irritated by having a shadow. I'd done this exact trek a hundred times before, but never as a protector.

That wasn't who I was.

My mother died when I was eight, and like Daze, I'd never known my father. I did whatever it took to keep myself alive. My life had been one giant on-the-job-training lesson. It was clear that Daze hadn't traversed that same road. He'd had a mother up until fairly recently.

We made it ten more stories. This building was the gateway into the canals, which was why my crew chose it as our entrance. The streets on the south side of this building had collapsed, filling in with water after the sea levels rose. The streets to the north were still intact, for whatever reason, and the incline higher. I didn't question anything anymore. It was here, so we used it.

On the twelfth-floor landing, I grabbed on to Daze's sleeve, dragging him forward, settling my ear against the door. He didn't make a peep, which impressed me.

No noise from the interior.

This old megascraper was a remnant of what the city used to be before the dark days, complete with all the fixings: interactive wall screens, solar window panels, bio-printers, and 3-D hologram capabilities, to name a few. But it wasn't so mega anymore. The top two hundred stories had been sheared off during the hurricane and gale-force winds that assaulted this city for weeks following the meteor strike, leaving only about thirty stories standing, which was actually fairly tall for this city. The average was between five and eight, although others were as high as fifty or sixty. Seekers occupied the top usable floors, but we'd secured the stairwell to the twelfth, which was why we were standing here.

I cracked the door, edging my helmet away from

my ear so I could listen. I had a noise amplifier in my pocket, but it was quiet enough for me to hear without it. I was tempted to pull out a phone and ask for a status report, but thought better of it. Staying off the grid was best for now.

Deeming it clear, I slipped through the opening, tugging Daze along with me.

We entered a long hallway that had once housed a business of some kind. I'd never, in all my years using this route, figured out what that business had been. Debris and trash littered the floor, like everywhere. Cleaning it up would've been an insurmountable task. A pile of rat feces sat on top of an old shoe to my right. Rats. They could survive anywhere. Too bad rat hide wasn't a usable staple. Neither was cockroach shell, although people had tried. Too brittle.

We reached the other end quickly.

This was where things got a little tricky.

I turned to Daze. "There's a steel beam out there"— I gestured vaguely behind me—"that will lead us from this building to the next. It's wide and sturdy enough to hold both your weight and mine, but there are zero handholds within your reach. You're going to have to hold on to me. You up for this?" It was a rhetorical question. He nodded, his too-large helmet sliding down and up over his forehead. He repositioned it with his hands. "Good. Follow me," I instructed. "I also advise that you not look down. Not that you'll see anything, because it's dark and murky, but keep your eyes on me and stay close."

Instead of following, Daze didn't move.

I glanced back. His eyes, which were the only part of his face I could see, were confused. Daze was in a daze.

Reaching inside my vest, I took pity on the kid, bringing out my trusty cord. Everything I needed for basic survival was tucked away in my vest someplace, as a pack was too cumbersome to lug everywhere. If I needed more, I had survival kits tucked away all over the city, stuffed with enough supplies to last me a week or more.

The cord was compact, yet strong. I'd salvaged it at least fifteen years ago. It was three meters long and less than two centimeters thick, made of something super strong and stretchy. Bender had deemed it my miracle rope. None of us had ever seen the likes of it before or after. We deduced it'd been left over from before the dark days, but nobody could be sure. Trinkets came and went, but this one was a staple.

I tied it around my waist, cinching it tight, handing the loose end to Daze.

When he didn't reach out to take it, I clutched his wrist, settling the cord inside his palm, curling my fingers around his, coaxing him to make a fist.

When that didn't work, I reached down and settled a hand on his shoulder, bending over to meet his unfocused eyes. "Do they call you Daze because you get dazed when you're worried?" I asked. He didn't answer. "Kid, I'm going to need you to snap out of it." I shook him lightly. "Daze, wake up."

He blinked a few times. "Yeah."

"'Yeah' is not good enough." I held back listing all the reasons why. "I need you alert and ready to move. Right now. Plunging to your death out there is not an option." I nodded over my shoulder toward the outside. "We're twelve stories up, and we just thwarted your demise a short time ago. Ending it now, by tumbling off a rafter, is a much less dramatic death than splattering yourself all over the gorge, but it would still achieve the same effect. You'd be dead. So, here, hold on to this end of the cord." I tied it around his wrist and stuffed the rest into his hand. "Now you're attached to me, and I'm attached to you. I'm not going anywhere. Your only job is to hold on." I stabilized the sides of his helmet with both hands, tilting it up so he had to look straight at me, careful not to slide it off his puny head. "Daze, honestly, this is the easy stuff. If you're going to survive in this city, you have to *want* to survive. From now on, everything we do is easy. If you let your brain get in the way, it won't work."

"Okay," he said in a thin voice.

"Okay, what?"

"I'll hold on."

"Is what we're doing easy or hard?"

"Easy."

"That's the spirit." I didn't give the kid time to reevaluate. Instead, I turned and headed around the corner, straight toward the gaping hole in the wall, a window with no glass, which was basically every window in the entire city. But this opening had a steel beam spanning the fifteen necessary meters to the next building.

I'd used it a million times before. We had no idea who originally put it there, but we'd happily commandeered it.

Every pathway we used in the city had been secured by me or my crew—meaning nobody else had access to our routes without breaking through some kind of barrier or encountering multiple security measures that would get them killed. Sometimes we used paint and symbols as warnings, just in case anybody became confused as to why they shouldn't go in, and sometimes we didn't.

On the rare occasion a route was compromised, we stopped using it until it could be secured again, or we moved to another location.

I stepped out on the steel, Daze shuffling in line behind me, his hands clutching my waist. I secured my grip on the long rope strung above our heads that was too high for Daze to reach. "I'm planning on traversing this quickly, so keep up."

I knew exactly how many steps I had to take to hit the end.

Twenty-three.

We were thirteen steps in when Daze's voice cracked. "Is that water below us?"

"I told you not to look down, kid." I sighed. It was a why-did-I-agree-to-sustainer exhale. "And yes, that's water. It glints a little off the metal in the dark."

"They say creatures live in the water," he said. "Big, scary serpents with knives for teeth and daggers for claws."

I chuckled. "Not sure who *they* are, but nope, no monsters in the water." I refrained from saying, *All the monsters you need to worry about live on land, kid,* but I didn't want to freak him out any more than he already was. I was nice like that.

Once at the end, I steadied Daze before I jumped down into the next building, reaching back to guide him by the elbow to make sure he made it with no stumbles.

"How do you know?" Daze asked as I untied the rope from my waist and his wrist and stuffed it back in my pocket. "Have you ever been in the water before? Like swimming in it?"

"I have, but that's not the reason I know." I scanned the hallway in front of us, my attention elsewhere. "You're not supposed to question me, remember? Come on. We have three more buildings to cross, and we're wasting time lingering."

Two steps in, a noise came from up ahead.

And just like that, my well-honed instincts took over.

Chapter 5

I wasn't used to reacting to a threat with company, but I made do. I had Daze out of the hallway and into a safe room in less than fifteen seconds. My crew and I tried to secure places on every floor of every building we used. Sometimes the space was a storage closet. Sometimes it was no bigger than a hollowed-out indent shielded by a removable wall. This one was an old office. One of the few that had a window to the outside. No glass.

This one provided an exit via a long cable that swung idly in the breeze, knocking softly against the building. I'd never had to use it before, but I was happy to see it. Before I could decide if we should make a quick exodus out said window, a tentative knock came from the door.

Not just any knock. It was a signal tap. One that indicated the coast was clear.

Meaning I knew this person.

Tat-a-tat-tat. Pause. *Tat-a-tat-tat-tat.*

"Holly, are you in there?" Darby's voice was strained.

I flung the door open with a confused look on my face as I hauled him inside, shutting it behind him. "What the hell are you doing here?" I whisper-yelled less than ten centimeters from his face. He shut his eyes against the spray of spittle, even though he was wearing a visor. Darby didn't venture out of his hole very often—and when I said not often, I meant never. He was our techie. He was kickass at his job, but hated life outdoors more than just about anyone I knew.

I hit a button on the bottom inside of my helmet, and low red light flooded around us so we could see each other better. We used red or blue light for almost everything, because it was harder to pick up at a distance. "Why are you here? Is there an emergency?" That was the only thing that would've gotten Darby out of his comfort zone.

"Well…" he hedged.

When he didn't readily offer anything up, I said, "Darby, enough with the nonverbal. What's going on?" I grasped him by the shoulders. "Tell me it's not Claire. Please let it not be Claire." When he didn't respond quickly enough, I shook him. My crew knew I wasn't good at bad news. It took me a while to shake it off.

Like, years.

"Everyone is fine," he assured me, turning on a small button light attached to his shoulder. A halo of blue blinked on. "The issue is…you. We were worried about you."

"Me?" I asked, dropping my arms and taking a step back. "Why me? I'm always out after blackout." Most of the time. "And I just talked with Bender on the phone."

"Yeah, but you didn't give him a signal indicating everything was fine."

"Why would I? We signal when things are shitty, not when things are solid."

"Yes, but he gave you the 'people are after you' tone."

"I know." I crossed my arms, starting to get defensive. "That's why I left Luce behind and headed here. I'm on my way to six."

"Six is good," he agreed. "But we thought maybe you were under duress, so you couldn't tell us what was really going on."

"Duress?" I wasn't someone who needed a babysitter. It was just the opposite—I cleaned up messes, I didn't make them.

"Well, because…" He angled his body to the side in an obvious slanting gesture, glancing around me, his eyebrows twitching. "The proximity monitors picked up two bodies." He shot me a pointed look. "Two means trouble, especially when everyone's accounted for. Who's your friend here?" He straightened and shoved his hands in his pockets.

"Oh, fuck." I tugged off my helmet, brushing my hair away from my face with an irritated hand. "You're right. I'm sorry. I didn't specify two." I didn't because

I'd never been a twosome before. Ever. "I made you leave your hole and everything." I smiled, playfully socking him in the shoulder. "But it was mighty nice of you to track me down here. Last time I checked, you were allergic to water, and you made it here so quickly. It does the heart proud."

Darby's gaze tracked to the floor. "I was…actually out anyway," he confessed. "I was just a few buildings away when Lockland made contact."

I folded an arm in front of me, my helmet dangling from my fingers, a soft red glow still radiating from inside. "You were out—as in out *out*, not just looking *out* your window or wistfully thinking about going *out*?" I'd never been to Darby's actual residence before. We kept our private lives private, because it was safer that way.

"Yes. I was out. I was going to tell you…" His voice trailed off, which was very Darby.

He wasn't ready to discuss his whereabouts, so I dropped it. For now. "Okay. Hanging around here is not advisable. I have to get Daze to six. The kid's exhausted, and I need to pump him for more information as soon as he wakes up." I turned and winked at Daze, who scowled back, his helmet in his hands, red issuing from it. He'd figured out the light. Smart kid. The headgear looked gigantic next to his small body. Mental note: Salvage a kid helmet as fast as possible.

"Daze, is it?" Darby asked, half to me, half addressing the kid directly.

"Yep," Daze answered back.

Darby smiled. "Man of few words. I like that." He addressed me. "I'm coming with you. It's too late to get home now…and I don't…enjoy blackout." He reached for the doorknob, but before he could open it, I smacked my palm against the cool metal, holding it shut.

I shook my head. "For safety reasons, you follow me, not the other way around. You make it into the canals maybe once a year, I do it weekly. I'm not used to working as a twosome—and certainly not as a threesome—but I'll figure it out." I glanced between the two so everyone knew where they stood. "We do this my way. Any complaints?"

Darby snatched his hand off the knob, having the decency to look abashed. "Of course not. You're totally right. I'm not used to this. You go first."

"We've accumulated too much time in here, especially since we just came from a building that houses seekers." Daze made a gurgling sound, which I pointedly ignored. I wasn't getting into another monster debate. "Sometimes they hear things and decide to check them out. They can't get through the barricaded stairway and would likely stumble off the beam if they tried to cross it, but it's been a long time since I reinspected either of these buildings. So, I go first, then I come back for the two of you." I held up a finger. "If I don't come back in ten—not twelve, *ten*— you take Daze out that window." I gestured to the wide-open space where slanted drizzle pelted the floor and the cable was busy bumping against the building. "Get back to Luce and contact Lockland. I have three spare tasers and whatever else you need in the back of the craft. He'll come get you." I donned my helmet, switching off the light. I didn't wait for Darby to respond, knowing he'd do exactly what I said. "Lock up behind me."

I slipped out the door. Crouching low to the ground, I listened.

This hallway was more exposed than the last one. At the other end, a small light was affixed to the wall covered by a screen. If Lockland had gotten wind of anything suspicious, the light would be red, and we'd be forced to go back the way we'd come, staying with Luce for the night.

I debated pulling out my tech phone, but there was a reason Bender and Lockland weren't choosing to use theirs. Either of them could've gotten a hold of me about the sensors picking up two bodies, but instead, they'd sent Darby.

This entire day was turning out to be unusual. Last time I had an unusual day, three people died. Two weren't my fault.

Halfway down, I backed myself into a large, square divot in the wall. It was most likely a space where a bio-printing meal machine had sat. Long before my time, the city had been mad for them. There were records that folks before the dark days had food and water aplenty, whenever and wherever they wanted it. No one ever went hungry.

Sounded like fucking utopia to me.

You couldn't find any actual machines anymore. They'd been either destroyed or given over to the government directly after the impact.

I leaned my head back against the wall and blocked everything else out, focusing on smell. I'd gotten good at detecting the telltale waft of a seeker. Since they spent their days either fogged or hunting for a fix, hygiene wasn't high on the list.

But it was more than that.

After ingesting a steady cocktail of pharma-psychotics for so long, they smelled toxic. It billowed around them like a cloud of noxious fumes. Their scent was actually similar to the all-purpose cleaner provided by the government called Bang. It was billed as a plague killer, and we were instructed to use it on everything.

A few more sniffs, and I deemed the air was free of noxious odor. I heard no surprising noises, so I ventured to the end of the hall. Once there, I removed the screen and saw the light was yellow.

As I watched, it began to blink.

Lockland was monitoring my movements. He knew where I was. This was a message to keep alert. We had a few live radar feeds that were strategically placed in the most dangerous areas. One of which was here.

Turning, I darted back down the hallway to the safe room and tapped on the door, giving the same sequence Darby had just used. As I waited for him to unlock it, I decided we weren't going to six. It was too far.

I had someplace closer in mind.

Darby cracked the door. "All clear?"

"For now," I said. "But we have to move. The light is blinking. Something must be up." I edged the door open with my shoulder, nodding at Daze to don his helmet, which he did quickly. Judging by his face, he was relieved to see I'd come back. Darby was as smart as they came, but didn't know tactics for shit. Following Darby across a steel beam must not have sounded appetizing.

Good, the kid had learned something valuable.

Daze hurried to my side, his helmet sliding sideways. His hands made the correction before it slipped completely off. "I heard a noise."

"Where?"

Daze gestured behind him. "Out that window."

I slid into the room. "Turn off your lights." Both Daze and Darby complied. I made my way to the edge, kneeling, moving debris to clear a space. I reached out and clasped the cold wet cable with a gloved hand and tilted my head out. We were too far up to hear anybody who might be maneuvering in the canal below. They didn't use boats, per se. More like makeshift rafts.

Then I heard it.

It was a light *schick-schick* of propellers. That meant it was nongovernmental. The ones the government used were big and loud. You could hear them rattling a kilometer away.

"Is it a UAC?" Daze whispered from behind me.

I stood. "Yep." The small ones weren't easy to detect. "And it's private. I haven't seen a privately operated one in these parts since the last time we flew ours." I nodded at Darby. "Have you?"

"Nope. Only two other groups have them that I know of," he answered. "None of them operate in the canals."

Why would they? Nothing to see here.

Unmanned aerial craft had been prevalent before the dark days. People used them for everything, including deliveries, surveillance, and protection. They came in all shapes and sizes and were so simple to use that a two-year-old could launch one and keep it in the sky. They ran by satellite-connected computer programs. Every caste had them.

Because of this, the dark city should have been littered with drone parts.

Except, directly after the impact, the government had asked early survivors to round up all the mechanical parts they could find—not only UACs, but also any remaining parts from robots or machines in general, including all 3-D printers. That was back when the government compensated people for contributing to the common good.

A few years ago, I'd been lucky enough to find a UAC with a working laser, which meant it'd been military grade. It was pretty badass. It resembled a small plane rather than a four-propped drone. We all agreed not to launch it in the city, as we didn't want to call attention to it unless we were under incredible threat, which thankfully hadn't happened yet. But we'd had some fun flying it in the scrub twenty kilometers outside city limits. Some of those trees had holes ripped through them the size of a trash bin.

"What does private mean?" Daze asked.

"It means someone other than the government is interested in us, which is never a good thing. This day keeps getting better and better," I grumbled as I stood, making my way toward the door. "New plan, we're heading to Mirabel. We need to exit this area before that drone picks up our heat signatures."

Chapter 6

"Are you sure you want to go to Mirabel, Hol?" Darby's expression was a cross between shock and curiosity. "Six is not that far."

"Yep. Let's move." Mirabel was one of my three private residences inside the city limits—at least the ones that were set up for everyday living. I had more spaces that I used as storage facilities and makeshift safe houses in a pinch.

Unlike one through seventeen, which were our shared, monitored safe places, Mirabel was mine alone, just as Darby had his own, and Claire, Bender, and Lockland had their own. I'd frequented Claire's and Bender's private residences. Claire lived in government-issued housing, since she worked for them, so nothing to hide there. And Bender's doubled as his workshop, where he was a sought-after mechanic and general wizard when it came to fixing gadgetry. Everyone in the entire city took what they needed repaired to his doorstep, which was how I'd stumbled on him coming up on nineteen years ago.

A long story with a fairly happy ending.

But I'd never been to Darby's or Lockland's residences. And no one had ever been inside Mirabel.

This was one weird day. It would forever be known as the day I scrambled my brain and got a kid.

Daze and Darby trotted after me down the hallway. Darby began to pant almost immediately. "Is your residence close by?" he huffed.

"Not used to aerobic exercise, huh, Darby?" I smiled. "It's only two buildings away." At the end, instead of heading out a window to another crossbeam, I pushed open a door, jamming my shoulder into it to clear the huge pile of trash that I'd heaped against it the last time I'd used this route. The stairwell was dark. "Head over to your right and grab on to the railing." I shut the door and kicked the pile of junk back against it. It made a clatter. "The trash will thin out the higher we go." There was less ambient light in here than in the hallway. Once the garbage was sufficiently stacked—enough to blockade a random seeker—I made my way to where the guys stood. "I'll take the lead. Don't get too far behind. Daze, want me to get out the cord?"

"No."

Good.

I had to boost myself over the initial heap of debris, and we began to climb.

"Lockland is going to be worried when he sees we

went off radar," Darby said as he tripped over a pile and swore, barely catching himself before he tumbled backward.

"Be careful," I warned. "It gets worse as we go, but then eventually clears." I crossed the first landing and started up again. "Three more levels and we can turn on our lights. All the doors the rest of the way up are secured. And, yes, Lockland will be wondering where we went. When we hit Mirabel, I'll let him know."

We traversed three more flights without mishap. Once at the top, I snapped on both my shoulder lights.

"That's a lot of garbage." Darby glanced around. He was right. It was everywhere.

"It keeps the seekers away." I shrugged. "They can't be bothered to pick their way through the stuff, so it works like a charm." The next few flights went slower as we made our way through even bigger piles, heaping so high that the steps were no longer visible.

"How many stories are like this?" Darby gripped the railing with both hands and hauled himself up as his feet tried to find purchase in the muck. The organic refuse had become dirtlike from decomposition over the years, aided by the constant wet environment. The rest of the chunks were metal and other nonbiodegradables.

It was a pile of nastiness.

The only good thing was it'd been so many years that it no longer carried a strong stench. The only bad thing was the noise. Once it was displaced, it tumbled all over the place, making a hell of a racket.

"Two," I called over my shoulder, glancing back to make sure Daze was okay. Kid was pulling himself up, hand over hand, using the railing like a rope, much more efficiently than Darby was.

Static erupted from inside my pocket.

Lockland was trying to figure out where we'd gone.

"One more to go," I told them as I plucked my phone out of my vest. I depressed the button twice, with the right number of pauses in between, letting him know we were fine, then stuffed it back in.

We rounded the top, and Darby came level with me on the landing, his chest heaving with effort. "How are we crossing to the next building?" he asked. "This is higher up than I usually go."

"A cable swing," I answered casually.

"You can't be serious," Darby said, wheezing.

"Totally," I replied. "It's actually one of my favorite ways to get around, especially in the canals. I've never been a fan of the steel-beam route."

"We don't use cable swings on our usual routes," he said. "Because they're too hard to attach, and they've been known to break. One bad swing and it's goodbye life."

"Not the way I do it. And stop scaring the kid." If I peered at Daze right now, the expression he'd be wearing would be a cross between worry and eye-popping fear.

"All this time," Darby huffed, "and you're a cable swinger. I always took you for a jetty."

"Jet packs and hoverboards are too loud." Once

upon a time, I'd seen a picture of a bicycle with a short description of how people used to use them. Jet packs and hoverboards were a good equivalent. But they weren't practical anymore. They ran on battery, coupled with liquid fuel, which was hard to find.

"True," Darby said. "But I've been working on a design to operate one solely on battery power." His tone became thoughtful. "But as of right now, the battery is too big, and the drag makes it too dangerous, even with extra props."

"Jetties were heavy to begin with." And cumbersome. The ever-present drizzle pattered on our helmets, as the stairwell roof had become completely open to the elements. "Kill the lights and stay here while I take a look. Nobody should be up here, because none of my traps have been tripped, but I want to double-check. Not to mention, make sure that UAC is nowhere nearby." I flipped off my shoulder lights. "And, Darby, can you do me a favor? Don't scare the kid by relaying horrible stories about death by cable swing."

"Not even one?" Darby asked. "Remember that guy—what was his name? Thom with an H? Or maybe it was Strohm with an H? He used to love cable swings until that time he jumped—"

"Cut it out." I slashed my hand down in a warning, trying not to laugh. "Now is not the time for you to make nice with your verbal skills. Keep your lips zipped and stay put. I'll be right back." I slipped out onto the roof, carefully stepping over a wire. I had trip wires all over the place, in addition to other things to help keep me safe. Booby traps were essential in our dark world. You had to know if anybody had gone before you.

I made my way to a shallow dome of mangled and twisted building struts and eased off my helmet, cocking my head to listen. There were tons of places to hide on the top of this building. Some buildings were laid bare, clear of any leftover building material, others were half sheared, leaving behind tall exposed beams, rebar, ceiling tiles, and other convenient places to tuck yourself away.

The air was free of any noise other than the never-ending drip of precip. Private drones were extremely rare. If this Tandor guy was behind the UAC searching for us, he wasn't kidding around. He'd hired me to find Daze, no mention of getting his valuable quantum drive back. There'd been an address for me to return the kid to, but now I knew all of it was bogus. He'd sent someone out to track me and the kid. When the Q7 went back empty-handed, they must've suspected that I'd taken the boy with me.

For Tandor to flaunt his technology showed his hand. He had access to a private UAC, a Q7, a quantum drive, and the ever-elusive pico. That meant he was heavily armed and thought he was smarter than the rest of us, likely undefeatable. That wasn't typical for a band of ragtag outskirts. They were usually sloppy and had access to lower tech.

When I was positive I couldn't hear any props, I

reached into my pocket and drew out my chromoscope glasses. The thick lens allowed me to see X-rays, ultraviolet rays, gamma rays—basically any and all rays. I scanned the top of the building, turning in a full circle, my finger clicking the lever as I went. It was habit to check the spectrum. Explosives, and the like, each had different color signatures in different wavelengths.

All clear.

I tucked the chromes back in my pocket and settled my helmet on. Then I went to retrieve the guys, motioning them out, while gesturing down at the wire.

They both stepped over it and followed me soundlessly toward the far corner of the roof. Daze was going to have to ride with me. There was no other way. I'd never gone two on a cable swing before, but I didn't have time to train him right now. It was a tricky thing to learn.

"Daze, we're going to watch Darby swing, then you and I go. There's nothing to be worried about." I stood on my tiptoes and unhooked the heavy cable attached to a mangled girder that jutted out high above the chasm in between the buildings. It'd taken me a week of hard work to get it secured exactly right. I'd risked my life shimmying up the girder in the rain, but it'd been worth it.

I walked toward Darby with the thing in my hand.

He took a step back, his hands going up in a surrender pose. "Whoa, the last time I was on one of these was when I was fifteen and running for my life.

I'm not sure I can do this." He glanced cautiously toward the other building.

I continued forward, nonplussed. "My swings don't fail." I reached into a pocket and pulled out my mag-hold. A ten-centimeter-long titanium tube with a hella strong magnet at each end. I attached it to the bottom of the cable. It suctioned on to the steel with a loud thunking sound. The only way to break the seal was by rotating the integrated air lever on the top. "Do you want to ride sitting or standing?"

"Sitting." His voice was resigned.

I wrapped the cable under his ass and stuck the other end of the mag-hold on to a section of cable above his head, creating a large, sturdy loop. "All you have to do is flick the air lever, rotate it forward, exactly two seconds after the next roof comes into view. It's easy. Remember to grab hold of the cable once you're down, then swing it back. And I don't have to remind you, Darby, there is no other way." I physically maneuvered him one hundred and eighty degrees around, directing him to the edge. "Ready?"

"Ready."

"Make sure you get sufficient momentum. Worst thing that can happen is you idle between the two buildings, but I can get you back. I have a hook, and if I have to break it out, I will."

Darby leaned backward, angling his body to get a decent takeoff, and bounced, propelling himself off the side.

Five seconds later, he crossed onto the next roof.

The buildings were roughly fifteen meters apart. I held my breath for the merest of seconds, willing him to unclip in time.

He did, dropping below the battered lip of the building. It was convenient that both of these buildings had been sheared off at about the same height. He stood, albeit a little wobbly, and walked to the edge, sending the cable back with a thrust of his arm.

I bent over, gripping the girder next to me, snatching the cable back. My hand coverings had micro-silia built into the fingertips to allow for gripping smooth surfaces in the rain. I turned to Daze. "See? That wasn't so bad."

"But…how are we going to do that together?" he asked. I was surprised to hear curiosity in his voice instead of fear. It seemed Daze preferred this way of travel better than the rafter route.

"I'm going to put it around my behind like so"—I showed him—"making sure it's super secure." I clipped it in a big loop around me and demonstrated that it wouldn't come apart. "And you're going to get on my back and hold on tight."

He shook his head. "If I do that, you might not be able to unclip, because I'll be in the way."

The urchin had a point.

I glanced down. I might be able to unclip, but Daze's legs could interfere with the success of the operation. "I suppose you could sit on my lap." I released the mag-hold and lifted it higher to create a big enough loop for us both to fit through.

Daze shook his head again. "That's just asking for trouble. You won't be able to reach the top if I'm on your lap."

I grinned. "So what's it gonna be, kid?"

"I'll ride by myself."

My eyebrows rose, which he couldn't see from inside the helmet, but they were up nonetheless. "That's pretty big talk from a boy who's never used a cable swing before. Think you can handle it?"

He tugged off his helmet and handed it to me. "I've never used one this big," he boasted. "But the street kids have all kinds of these all over the city."

"Well, then." I moved forward, cinching the cable under his body and attaching the mag-hold much lower than I had for Darby. "I'm making the loop big for a reason. Instead of unclipping, just slide out." The air lever took some strength to flick. Daze sat on the cable, testing it. "Grab the top here with both hands," I instructed, "and don't let go until you see the roof. Once it comes into view, count to two. If your timing's off, don't panic. I can hook you back. Panic never gets the job done."

"Got it," he replied confidently. "But I gave you my helmet, so I don't have any way to see." A wobbly helmet wasn't going to help this situation.

I plucked my chromoscope glasses back out of my pocket and placed them across the bridge of his nose. "I love these more than Luce, so don't fall through the loop before your eyes land on the prize. I'm not fishing them out of the canal. That would be a huge hassle." I flicked the dial to infrared.

He gave me a thumbs-up, and I walked him backward, then rushed forward, hurtling him toward the next building, praying he didn't slip to his death. I watched as he swung out over the dark crevasse, not realizing I'd steepled my hands in front of my face, counting to two in my head once he reached the other side.

He let go, sliding from the loop at just the right time.

The kid had guts.

Chapter 7

"If I never see another swing, I'll die a happy man," Darby muttered. We'd just landed on my building, having taken another ride to get here.

"Don't be such a child," I teased as I hooked the cable to a piece of metal, so it would be ready for the ride back. "Especially when the kid just kicked your ass, establishing himself as a swing pro. That one was a tiny one compared to the first one. And look, we're here." I took the lead, handing Daze his helmet. "I go first. You two copy everything I do."

"How many traps are we looking at?" Darby asked. "And how many of them are fatal?"

"Too many to count," I replied. "And all of them." I didn't mess around with security at my residences. "Just do what I do, and everyone lives." I tapped Daze on the shoulder. "Oh, and I need my chromes back." I held out my hand.

The kid slid them off reluctantly, setting them in

my open palm. They were certainly a better fit than his helmet. "That was cool," he responded enthusiastically. I assumed he was referring to the cable swings and not the glasses. Although, the chromes were super cool and hard to come by.

"A swing lover," I said, rolling my helmet visor into the housing then donning my chromes, clicking them to X-ray. "It must be your lucky day. I have another pair inside. Two of the dials are broken, but I'm happy to lend them to you." He gave me a cheesy grin, which looked comical through my lenses. Teeth all day. "Follow me. And I'm not kidding—do everything I do and don't touch anything if you value functioning hands and feet."

Mirabel was my primary residence, since the canals took effort to get to on a regular basis for most people. It was my favorite for several reasons. One, it was named after my mother, and almost everything I had from our time together was stored here. When I was little, my mom didn't go out much, so I didn't either. But every once in a while, before the canals were overrun by seekers, my mother would bring me here. She'd grown up in this building. Unlike the other buildings around, which housed offices and manufacturing centers, this megascraper had been luxury condominiums, with all the bells and whistles. Integrated wall screens, state-of-the-art sleeping pods, 3-D personal printers that could print anything you needed, solar-capture windows, as well as full terraces that had been used for growing supplemental food.

These megascrapers had been completely closed systems. They'd recycled everything from gray water to waste efficiently and generated their own power with solar windows and wind turbines on the roof.

Two, I kept most of my prized loot here, because it was the most defendable location I had. Even the government didn't want to deal with the seekers and outskirts who came here.

Three, the building had been sheared off at fifty stories, so it was one of the tallest still standing. Over the years, I'd amassed more solar panels than I was fairly certain anyone had. So, this was where I charged my batteries necessary for life. All life.

Everything we did required batteries.

If it hadn't been for the invention of nano-helium, just before the dark days, we'd have nothing—no power, no tech, no communication. Some genius—and I meant that in the most literal sense—invented a super-efficient battery that could store power at the atomic level, and if he hadn't, the world would be stone-cold extinct by now. Shallow light constantly filtered through dismal cloud cover, and the rocks and debris that orbited Earth, but it was enough to keep the batteries limping along.

The best time for charging was around the summer solstice, when we had the longest days of the year. The city made a point of charging up during solstice.

I scanned the roof with my chromoscopes, noting that my tarps were all in place, none of my ultraviolet markers disturbed.

Beside me, Darby cleared his throat. "Are those…"

"Yes." I continued my search of the roof. "Panels. Lots and lots of panels. It took me a full year to sew all those tarps together to make them look like they'd been haphazardly scattered there. That way, any government UACs or surveillance interested in this area never detects them." I uncovered them only when I could monitor everything.

It was highly illegal for an individual to own more than two panels or have more than two operating solar windows. We were supposed to hand the surplus over to the government so they could power their own buildings, and fuck the rest of us.

I had fifty-three.

"You always have charged batteries," Darby commented. "But you never talked about why. Now I get it."

I clicked my glasses to the next setting as I moved forward, stepping over deliberately placed stacks of junk. "The less you knew the better. If the government got a hold of you and injected you, you'd be guilty by association."

Darby fell in line behind me. "I have it on good authority they've run out of the dreaded Babble."

My eyes tracked in a grid, making sure every signal light I had was still lit, as we made our way toward my hatch. "I heard the same rumor." I exaggerated my leg movements over a wire so the guys noticed. "Some time last year, the vials ran dry. But they're keeping it hush-hush. Claire had no idea." Claire worked as a liaison to child welfare within the government. That's how we'd met. I was a street kid in distress, and she'd been an adult who gave a shit. "That's why you're here, Darby. We can afford to be a little lax when the government doesn't have access to Babble."

Babble, invented before the dark days, had shut down the need for public trials for a time. Once a person was injected, they lapsed into unconscious verbal memory—answering any question truthfully—and once they woke, they had no recollection of what they'd confessed. A talented investigator could pull memories from birth to present day, and the entire confession was public record. Nothing in your past was free from prosecution, either. So, once brought in for one crime, all the other shitty things you did were up for grabs.

That era had been documented as a blissful crime-free time in our world. But in subsequent years, the government had been faced with violent protests and rampant suicide from those who'd rather die than have their past laid out for the world to see.

After that, Babble became highly regulated.

It hadn't been originally named Babble—it'd been labeled something like Articulation Interrogation Serum. But after the dark days, it was nicknamed Babble, because that's all anyone did on it. Babbled about their sorry, awful lives.

If you were injected with the memory extractor now, you were basically guaranteed a death sentence, because everyone here had broken the law in some way.

My fifty-three solar panels were the *least* of my infractions.

The first time I'd broken the law, that I could remember, I'd been six years old. I'd crawled into an abandoned apartment and found a pixie motor. I knew it was something I should turn over to the government, but instead I stuck it in my pocket, not even telling my mother.

I still had it.

To this day, pixies were hard to find. They were small, ultra-efficient motors, drawing only a tiny amount of current, and were interchangeable in a ton of things. So much so, the government still required us to turn them in.

Not that I did, but it was mandated.

I skirted another trap.

This one was a canister of tasespray, aimed to send an arc of gas released at ultra-high pressure straight at an attacker's face. Back in the Carbon Max era—some two hundred years prior, before bio-innovation and NewGen technology—it was called tear gas. But if you fell victim to tasespray, not only did your eyes burn like hell, you were blinded for a solid forty-eight hours, along with the warm, cozy feeling of gigantic needles inserted straight into your retinas.

I knew firsthand, unfortunately.

Tasespray was not my friend.

I'd never met a single person who hadn't been completely incapacitated by a dose to the eye, even a seeker in full rage-mode. Even though they were desperate for a fix, they could feel pain—and were said to be especially sensitive since their pleasure receptors were overly enlarged. Tasespray was one of the government's favorite standbys, but there were rumors that they were running low on this, too, so the horizons were looking brighter and much less painful.

The three of us made it to the northwest quadrant of the roof without managing to set off any of my security measures. I stopped, placing a knee on the ground, hefting up a large square of what looked like steel.

I lifted it easily.

That's because it wasn't steel.

It was synthetic simulation board, three times lighter. I motioned for Daze to come forward. "I'm going to drop you in first," I told him. "Once you're down, stand still and wait for us." He nodded without question. He sat on the edge, and I took his arm, releasing him down the three meters to the hallway below.

I motioned Darby to go next. "I'm impressed, Hol. There's no question that you've always been badass, but this is on an entirely different level. The scope of what you have here is awesome. We've got a lot to discuss."

"Does that mean you're inviting me to your place for dinner and drinks?"

His face went pensive for a second. "I think I am. With your solar capacity and my power grid, the implications are vast. We might be capable of achieving something even the government hasn't been able to do before…"

"Loss for words right at the reveal." I chuckled. "So very like you, Darb. Now get down there. We have more important things to discuss."

"What could possibly be more important than massive amounts of power?" he asked as he plunged into the opening.

I leaned over, grinning. "A quantum drive and the possibility of recovering an intact pico." I took massive pleasure watching Darby's face go from surprise, to shock, to wonder, in less than three seconds. His mouth was still gaping as I dropped through the hole next to him.

"You can't be serious." He tugged off his helmet, his short brown hair sticking up in hunks all over his head, wet and sweaty. That's what wearing a helmet twelve to fourteen hours a day did. It made you a stinky, hot mess.

"As serious as tasespray to the eye." I shimmied up to the ceiling, using the strategic spots I'd placed in the wall to drag the trapdoor shut. Once it was firmly in place, I locked it from beneath with a steel deadbolt bigger than my fist.

Jumping back down, I clapped the wet and grime off my gloves. Then set my chromes to infrared, dragging my gaze across the hallway, searching for any unusual heat signatures. "All clear," I said. "Follow me, and I shouldn't have to remind you not to touch anything, so this is your nonreminder."

Partway down, I doffed my helmet and set my ear against the wall. There was no way anyone could get to this floor without coming through the hatch, but it was always good to be thorough. I'd inserted a sonic-wave module in the wall. If anybody was moving around inside my unit, it would emit a low-level hum.

No noise.

I continued a few more meters, muscling an upended cooling unit out of the way, revealing not so much a door as a steel wall. One that looked to have no hinges or doorknobs. I peeled off my glove and set my open palm in the upper right quadrant.

After a moment, there was a pop, and the wall cracked open a centimeter.

Darby made a sound of disbelief, that came out like a partial sob-cough. "Why didn't you tell me you have heat-sensor technology?" His tone projected equal parts hurt and wonder. Darby and I had never had serious tech talks, so he had no idea how much I actually had or knew. Most of the time we communicated via phone. Visits were scarce, and we had group meetings only once every three to four months. Socializing was a luxury most of us didn't have.

I nudged the door open a crack with the tip of my boot, listening, scanning the slim view of the interior that I could see. "The same reason you haven't told me you have a working retinal-recognition display." The technology for both heat and retina had become orphaned after the dark days, with no new manufacturing or engineers to operate it. I'd come across a few heat-sensing pads a number of years ago and put them to good use. Now was not the time to tell Darby that Bender and Lockland were fully aware I had them, and Bender had been the one to modify and get them working.

But the boys had no idea where I'd installed the pads. That was the key.

"Touché," he said. "But how do you know about…"

"I'm the one who actually leaves my home, remember?" Although I hadn't seen the inside of Darby's residence, I'd been to the outside many times. He lived near a passage I used often, right on the inside of Government Square. I ushered the guys in and shut the wall behind us, depressing a lever that engaged a complicated system of interlocking spirals, resembling a web. It connected together at the end with a loud, grating thunk.

Once that was done, I strode into the entryway, simultaneously hitting a switch to shut down motion sensors and turn on the lights. The entire condo had voice-recognition capabilities back in the day, but they were all defunct now. I tugged my glasses off and set them, along with my helmet, on the utility ledge that ran around the entire space. The apartment was streamlined and glossy white. Bang kept the surfaces gleaming.

"Everyone can relax," I said. "If any threats come within thirty meters of this place, I'll know it." I peeled off my other glove and tossed both down next to my chromes and helmet.

Next, I unzipped my vest, while simultaneously reaching out to press a single fingertip into an integrated panel on my wall. It sprang open.

Daze exclaimed excitedly, pointing to my waist as I shrugged off the vest, "Is that a Gem laser? I've never seen one up close. Those are so cool."

I hung my attire—chock full of its life-saving weapons and tech—on a hook inside the storage locker that contained an arsenal of even more weapons and shut it up safe and sound. It would open only for my fingerprint. "It is, and for now you will remain a Gem virgin. My gun is temperamental, and I only bring it out when the situation calls for it. One thing at a time, kid."

Chapter 8

Daze trailed behind me as I made my way in to my compartmentalized living space. "Is that a full tase on your waist? Or a half?" he asked. "And what's in that other holster? Is that a handgun? Does it shoot actual bullets? I've never seen one before. I thought they were made up."

My vest contained a multitude of useful items, but I kept the necessary ones strapped to me at all times. Two guns and one taser at my waist, a knife strapped to each thigh, and other things attached to various body parts, none of which Daze was getting an eyeful of anytime in the near future.

I tapped on more lights.

Everything in this place was protected from the outside. The windows were covered in thick graphene. I stopped in front of my big screened wall, turning to the kid. "Yes, it's a full taser set to Most Pain Inflicted, or MPI, as I like to say. It will stun and drop the biggest adult you've ever seen. And yes, it's a handgun, but it doesn't shoot the bullets you're talking about. People love to gossip, but that kind of technology hasn't been around for more than a hundred years." I patted the cold steel hugging my hip. "This shoots air bullets filled with Nyoxine gas. The air bubbles, once in your bloodstream, kill you by blowing up your heart. The gun runs on vaporized fuel. Don't touch it."

Daze's face was a mixture of awe and super awe. I'd just morphed into this kid's walking, talking idol.

Darby came in after us, taking everything in. "This is incredible," he murmured, pacing directly toward the far wall. I knew he would. He took off his gloves and began to trace the contours of the packs mounted there. He turned to me, his eyes bright. "How many?"

"I lost count around eight hundred and something." I opened my cooling unit and drew out a jug. Water in this building, before the dark days, had been recycled in an efficient hydroponic biosphere, back when these luxury apartments ran smoothly. Now I piped it in from the roof, running it through a reverse-osmosis system. It still tasted a bit metallic because of the iron, but it was drinkable.

I'd been lucky that this entire building had been wired for a backup power source in case of global calamity. Kudos to the architects. Powering that closed circuit with my batteries made running the cooling unit, lights, and everything else possible. I still could've achieved it, but that made it easy.

Darby's eyes tracked back to the wall, and his hand went up again, seemingly without his permission.

"Darby, stop fondling my batteries," I teased as I opened some cabinets—these were integrated, but not fingerprint sensitive—and drew out three cups and poured the cool liquid in.

Once they were full, I put away the jug and grabbed the remote sitting on a shelf and pointed it at the wall, clicking a button.

The micro-pixelated screen that ran the span of the entire room sprang to life.

"Whoa," Daze half wheezed as he stumbled forward, extending his arm. Even Darby was momentarily distracted from my power-packed wall. "Is that…a mountain?" Daze's helmet was long gone. The kid squinted, rubbing his eyes, much like I had when I'd first taken in the same scene. The video was so much brighter than anything we were used to seeing on a daily basis, it was almost blinding.

"It is." I walked the two cups over, handing one to Daze and the other to Darby. Even if I snapped my fingers in front of both of their faces, it wouldn't have broken the spell.

Mirabel wasn't a typical residence.

Darby didn't make a move to drink his water. Instead, his eyes found mine, confusion and surprise in them. He was at a loss for words. So very Darby.

"It's a looped video feed, as far as I can tell," I said. "I just discovered it about a year ago. I thought the screen was dead, but when I was rooting around in the wall, inserting another sonic-wave monitor, I came across some wires that I hadn't seen before. I fixed them, joining them to my closed circuit"—I shrugged—"and this popped to life."

Darby made a sound in the back of his throat. It was a cross between a gurgle and snort. He moved to stand next to Daze, the two of them equally mesmerized by the larger-than-life mountain, with its clear blue backdrop, swaying, lush green trees, and pristine snowcap.

I'd done the same thing.

In fact, I'd lost track of the hours I'd spent in front of it.

Darby finally turned and said simply, "I'm glad Babble is gone."

I chuckled. "Me, too." Or Darby wouldn't be here, watching this video. The kind of everyday convenience our ancestors had taken for granted. They'd been able to set the screen to any channel they wanted, at any time. They likely had access to live streaming as well. People loved to live-stream animals, according to the records. Watching them around the clock in their natural habitats was a particular favorite. I took a sip of water, clasping my arm around Darby's shoulders. "Forgive me for not telling you," I murmured in his ear. "If anyone had known, they would have insisted on coming to see. And with my wall of illegal batteries, coupled with my vast cache of illegal solar panels and everything else against the law I have stored here, I couldn't risk it. Acid baths are not a favorite of mine."

Darby cracked a smile. "I forgive you. I'm just happy to be here right now. This is…incredible. I have no words. Most of the superscreens left are damaged. Very few, if any, work. It's due to their old-fashioned technology. The fluid pixels that make up this screen have a limited life-span. This"—he gestured toward the green, mountainous scene—"in theory should've dried up a long time ago."

"Well, I'm glad it didn't." I glanced around my small but adequate living space. "I'm proud of this place. It only took me eight years to clean it up, secure it, and make it livable." Eight years, in the scope of things, was a short time span. Anything worth doing took years. "There's a sleeping space on the other side of the entryway and a semifunctioning waste room, and that's it."

Darby nodded, pivoting his head around, taking it all in. "My place only has one room. This is a castle compared to most."

"My two other residences are much smaller," I said. "In fact, one is no bigger than a glorified closet. I have nothing incriminating in it, and I keep it because it's in a convenient location, right inside Government Square. It's the only one I list legally." The government required you to have an address on file, or you didn't get your protein blocks. I drained my water, setting the cup on a table attached to the integrated bench below the screen.

Darby lifted his glass to his lips and took a long drink. Daze still hadn't made a peep. His eyes were locked on the screen, his mouth hanging open. He was mesmerized.

I clicked a button on the remote, and the screen slowly morphed into a new scene. Anticipating Daze's reaction, I bent over and plucked the cup from his hand before he dropped it. "Is that…a horse?" he asked, shuffling a step closer, his other arm still semi-raised. He hadn't gotten around to relaxing it yet.

"I'm impressed, Daze," I said. Knowing your animals wasn't a given. Most had been extinct for years. "It is indeed a horse. As the video continues, you get to see more of them. I'm surprised you know the name of this animal on sight. People used to ride around on their backs." The horses in front of us fed on rolling hills of emerald-green grass. The video was obviously shot with a UAC. As the drone floated downward, it presented the viewer with different sweeping angles.

It was completely mystifying that our world ever looked like that. It was hard to imagine. And it was sad. It represented everything this place could've been, but wasn't.

Daze turned to me, jutting his chin out, making it clear that my underestimating him was getting old. "Along with pictures on the walls, there were old books. Someone said the place we stayed at used to be a library, whatever that was. I've seen lots of animals. My mom taught me to read. She was good like that."

"With a pico lying around, I hope reading is not all you learned."

"The pico was my dad's," he replied glumly. Then he grinned, lifting his gaze to mine. "My mom said he was an expert."

My eyebrow went up. "An expert at what?"

Daze looked confused. "I'm…not sure."

I ruffled his hair. "That's okay, kid. I have a hunch we'll find out soon enough." I took him by the shoulders and guided him gently away. He resisted, but only a little, his feet finally catching up with his torso. "You can come back and check out the other videos later. But first you need sleep. I'm going to put you in the cleaning unit, get some protein in you, and then put you to bed. Because that's what sustainers do." I couldn't believe I was a sustainer. "They call the shots, and the sustainees follow their every command without question."

"What are the other videos of?" Daze asked on the end of a yawn.

"One is of a single white building. The only interesting thing about that one is the white, billowy clouds and rich blue sky. I could watch those clouds whisper over that building all day. You might like the other one, but it annoys the hell out of me. It's a bunch of bees. I have no idea why someone would order that for their screen, but there are some pretty-colored flowers in the mix. The buzzing gets old fast."

"Bees?" Darby asked, following us.

"Yes. At least I think they are. Black and yellow bodies, clear wings, annoying sound that feels like it's boring into your temporal lobe."

"They were a big deal before the dark days," he said. "One of the reasons the powers that be were forced to integrate 3-D bio-printing everywhere faster than technology was ready was because bees were becoming extinct. Without them to pollinate fruits and vegetables, things they relied on heavily for sustenance, people were starving."

"Good to know," I said. The government had some of our history on file, all the stuff that survived. You could access it at any time. But if it wasn't about technology, and furthering my own personal life expectancy, I wasn't apt to have learned about it. I had a rudimentary knowledge about things like horses and bees.

"I'm a bit of a nature buff," Darby admitted sheepishly. "Especially stuff from before the dark days. Unlike you, I'm always at home. I've found a lot of audio programs over the years that I can listen to with my net-adapted speakers. It's not as good as having video, but it works."

Beeping erupted from three places in my apartment at once.

My tech phones were going off.

I swore under my breath, veering Daze into the waste room. "Get the kid into the cleaner stall and press the green button," I instructed Darby. "I forgot to get a hold of Lockland. He'll send out the cavalry if I don't respond within thirty seconds."

He and Bender made up the cavalry, and it would take them hours to get here, but, as always, it was the thought that counted.

Chapter 9

I plucked a phone off the shallow indent next to my sleeping unit. "Jerry, it's Ella," I said as I depressed the button. This phone was black and sat in the palm of my hand. "Are you free tomorrow for breakfast?"

Static came over the line first, then, "No can do. But I'm available for lunch."

"Sounds good, I'll meet you at Seventh Street, midday," I said. "Sweet dreams."

"Over."

That's all it took to let him know I was safe.

I set the phone back down and walked into the waste room. Bathtubs and traditional showers for pleasure had been obsolete for ages, even though along my travels I still encountered remnants of them here and there. I had no idea why people chose to immerse themselves in water for hours at a time. The notion didn't even compute.

Water had been radically conserved before the dark

days. It'd been meant for drinking and watering plants. In its place, bio-cleaning stalls had been invented. They were designed as a closed system, like everything else manufactured in the twenty-second century.

A shallow water reservoir sat at the bottom of the stall and held no more than four liters of liquid. It was superheated instantly to produce steam, and once you were sufficiently beaded with sweat, cleanser was diffused from various nozzles. You lathered your body, and then sprayers, focused in short bursts, doused you for the end result, followed by a quick fan to dry you off.

It worked like a charm, and once you were done, the water and cleanser were purified and recycled, ready for next time.

The entire ordeal took under three minutes.

Darby shook his head as I came in. "I can't believe you have a working cleaning stall. I'd kill for one of these. I have a handheld sprayer. It's not the same."

I leaned against the wall, crossing my arms. Darby had stripped Daze of his clothing, down to his undergarments, and the kid was inside the cleaner looking around wide-eyed as the walls misted with steam. "When the cleanser comes, use your hands to scrub it in," I told him as I turned to Darby. "It took me some time to wire this thing up, but I lucked out all around with this place."

"I'll say." Darby gestured to the commode. It was simple and unordained. It was the standard model in most megascrapers. "That looks like a chem-toilet. Does it work?"

"It wasn't a chem to start with." I lifted the lid, showing him the bubbling green solution in the bottom. "Until I made it one. Originally, this was linked to the building's system, like everything else. All components recycled once flushed. The solid waste became fertilizer, and the wastewater went through reverse osmosis. You know the drill. I managed to run a pipe through the wall in the back that injects breakdown fluid into its holding unit. It works well enough."

Darby nodded thoughtfully. "I have something similar, although my building wasn't as technically advanced as yours to begin with. It was awaiting an upgrade before calamity struck." He turned back to the cleaning stall. Daze was in the process of being sprayed off. "If you ever see one of these while you're out and about, let me know. It would be cumbersome to relocate, but I'd pay good money for one. I'm fairly certain I could make it work in my space, even if you brought it to me in pieces."

"Will do," I said.

The door on the stall popped open after the drier ran for a minute, and I handed Daze a square of cloth. I was running low. Fabric of any kind always sold well. The kid took it and dried the lingering liquid out of his hair, mopping his face. I was pretty sure he was blond, instead of brown like I'd originally thought, but I'd have to wait until his hair dried to be certain.

"That was so cool." Daze's eyes shone, along with the rest of him. I'd been right, he was actually pretty cute with all the grime gone. He still looked like an eight-year-old, though. He was short and slight, bones sticking out all over the place. The kid needed food, and plenty of it. "The only cleaning stall I ever saw before was in my mom's friend's apartment. But she never let me use it. She said it was only for special occasions." Daze flashed a disgruntled upper lip at the memory.

I chuckled. His game face was A-plus. "You clean up good, kid. I'll toss your garments in a solution wash. We need them to function until we can get you new ones." I had nothing that would come remotely close to fitting him. "They'll be clean and dry in the morning—well, clean-ish. Not sure anything stronger than Bang will take out that ground-in dirt." I plucked the threadbare clothing off the floor with two fingers, wrinkling my nose. "And you were worried about *my* stinky stuff? What did you do, roll around in puddles every day?" I slid a container out from the wall and dropped the garments inside, punching a button on the lid.

"You have an integrated washing unit?" Darby said. "This place just gets better and better."

"The entire room was on one circuit, so when I made it work, everything operated. Just like the cleaning stall, the washing unit recycles itself. It's stand-alone. This building was cutting-edge."

"Well, it's better than what most of us can do. I use a bucket of cold drizzle and a couple of shots of cleanser."

I steered Daze into the next room. "The sleeping unit is heated to adjust to your body temperature. You'll be comfortable in there as is." He didn't argue as I walked over to a lever on the wall and tugged. A long tube emerged. These used to be voice activated, but I was just thankful I could get them open. The room held two units, two meters apart. I'd never needed the spare until today. I addressed Darby, who was watching with rapt curiosity. "Can you go get the kid a protein cake? I have some in the cooling unit."

He nodded. "Sure thing."

After he left the room, I finished rolling the thing out and lifted the clear lid. "Get in," I instructed Daze. It was made for a large adult-sized body, so there was plenty of room. "Once I close this, the top will become opaque. Don't worry, you can always get out. Just punch this button near your head." I indicated the location of the switch as Daze crawled in.

"I've seen one of these before." He turned over to lie down. "They had a few at the library." He looked incredibly tiny in the vast space. I could climb in there with him and have enough room, no problem.

"They're fairly common." I nodded. Most new and upgraded buildings had them. "When the lid is secure, the heat will kick on. It'll take a few minutes. I'm programming the cycle for twelve hours, because it looks like you could use some solid sleep. It wakes you up by ultraviolet light, which, according to the directions I found, is supposed to mimic a sunrise, but we can only take their word for it. The light eases itself on, going from pink to orange to yellow, gathering in brightness. I want you to stay in there until it clicks off. Keep your eyes shut, even if you wake up. Too much UV on the retina and you're blind. It looks like you haven't been under a lamp in months, so you need it. You know, it's dangerous to go without for so long. The wake-up cycle runs approximately twenty minutes. We clear?" Without manufactured ultraviolet light, the human race wouldn't have survived. Just one more thing on the *thank goodness we have it or we'd be dead* list. It was lucky things like these had already been integrated before the dark days hit.

"Clear," Daze replied. The kid looked beat, his eyes barely managing to stay open. He'd be asleep before the lid fully engaged.

Darby walked in and handed the urchin a protein cake, while nibbling on one himself. "These aren't too bad." He brought it out in front of him to inspect it. "Meat-and-potato-flavored is my guess."

I snorted. "I believe that one is supposed to be lemon pie." All the flavors were arbitrary to us anyway, since we'd never had the real thing to compare it to.

Darby took a sniff. "I do detect a hint of lemon. I don't know why they can't get it right. It shouldn't be that hard if they have the appropriate slurry. Atoms form molecules, molecules form food."

"It's the machines," I said. The 3-D bio-printers on the scale the government needed were wonky at best. "Claire said they've been trying to get it right for years, but the machines won't cooperate, and nobody knows how to fix them. So, instead we get"—I angled my head at the cake—"that."

Daze took the food, and I began to shut the lid. His arm shot up at the last second. "Holly?"

"Yes?"

He angled his tired head up. "Thank you."

"You bet." His tone said it all. It'd been a mixture of something that made my eyes soften and my heart clench. So, damn, I guess I'd been right the first time. The thing had decided to work again against my better judgment. "We have a lot to discuss in the morning. The plan is for us to go to Port Station to see if we can find your dad's old pico, so I want you to try to remember everything you can about where you used to live. It's going to be a risky endeavor, but I know you can handle it. After all, if you can master a cable swing in one try, this will be easy."

He nodded as he took a bite of his food. "Don't worry. I remember it all. My mom always said I had a memory as good as an adult, even when I was small."

"Alrighty then. Good night. I'll see you in the morning." I shut the top and punched in the code, setting the thing for twelve hours like I'd promised. The lid fogged immediately.

At the time of their invention, these sleeping pods were created to achieve the best rest possible, with a contoured air particle support system beneath you that inflated and deflated automatically as you moved. It was always exactly the right temperature, adjusting as you slept, with an extra influx of oxygen, and the aforementioned ultraviolet wake-up setting. It could even pipe in your favorite music, and the area right above your head was a screen. Nothing had been programmed into these units, but I liked to imagine the person who used to live here had enjoyed watching their favorite programs before they went to sleep.

I usually slept with my lid open. I wasn't the trusting sort.

Darby and I moved out of the room, making our way back to the living area. The horses were still roaming on emerald grass, grazing away, flicking their tails with no idea of what was to come.

"This is truly incredible." Darby headed straight for the battery packs along the wall. Each battery cluster was made up of ten or more circular nano-helium batteries, with a conduit running directly to the solar panels through the ceiling. "How much power does it take to run this place?"

I went to the cooling unit and took out a protein cake for myself. I had at least twenty inside and two other cooling units on this floor alone. I used my extra coin to make sure I had more than enough food. "Less than you'd think." I took a bite. They tasted awful, but apparently were engineered with all the vitamins and nutrients we needed. "Everything that runs in the unit is linked to that wall via those cables to your right. I spread out the use, so I never drain any one pack completely."

"I can't believe that you've amassed this many." He

shook his head. "And I thought I had a lot. But my packs number in the low hundreds."

I finished off the cake, dusting my fingers off on my pant leg. They were always a mess. "Come with me." I gestured, heading toward the entryway. "As long as you're here, I might as well show you everything. If you enjoyed the batteries, you're going to love this." I swiped my chromes off the shelf and went to disengage the web lock, laying my ear on the wall next to the door. Once I was certain the hallway was clear, I placed my palm on the cold steel.

Once we were out, I shut it, locking it up again with my hand. Heat-sensor technology was incredibly simple. All it took to open the door was a local change in temperature. You just had to know where to apply it. Since not many had access to the technology, it was fairly foolproof.

"We're not going outside, are we?" Darby glanced around. The hallway was long and dark and carried mold-scented undertones, like most things around here. It was part of the fabric of the environment when it rained damn near constantly.

I put on my chromes. "No. Well, not technically. I guess it depends on your definition of outside." I adjusted the dial to infrared and moved forward. Halfway down the hall, I stopped in front of a regular-looking door. I set my ear to it and turned the knob, easing it open. "My unit had access to a shared balcony. This is the entrance." We went through a short passageway. "Close the door behind you and engage the big bolt." I drew my Gem out of my belt, just in case anyone was lurking.

One blast from this, and they would have a large hole burned straight through them.

The balcony was secure from the inside, but it was impossible to lock it down from the outside. We were fifty-some stories up, so the likelihood of someone being out here was rare. But that didn't mean people couldn't be tricky if they found out what I had up here.

I pressed my finger to my lips, indicating Darby should move cautiously. Because of the wind and rain, it was too hard to hear. When I didn't detect any movement, I eased around the corner.

Darby followed.

On the balcony, I stepped to the side, giving him a full, unimpeded view of one of my most-prized possessions. It wasn't that big, but what it produced was worth its weight in coin. Through infrared, it wouldn't look as spectacular as it would during the day, but we were here now.

"Holy shit…" Darby stumbled toward my E-unit, his hands extended in front of him like a seeker. "Is this…an electrolysis system?" He snapped his head toward me to see my answering nod, his eyes wide. "Is it open or compressed?"

"Compressed." I joined him as he stood by the machine, ogling it. "The hydrogen comes out in condensed nano-carbon cubes." The pleasure I took in introducing Darby to my fuel lab took me by surprise. I'd kept it secret for so long, it felt strange to out myself, but also fantastic at the same time. I'd put a lot of hard work into this. I plucked one of the pellets out of the bin, making sure to hold on to the sides carefully. The gas was stable in the cell, but dropping it would be bad. Any blast of energy could cause it to explode. It wasn't more than a centimeter square. "When needed, the gas can be extracted with pressurized canisters to use as fuel, the cubes reused. Just like the ones Lockland gives us, but I found a ton more. Or they can be placed in a gun that uses vaporized fuel." When Darby didn't respond, I elbowed him. "Now's a good time to be verbal. What do you think?"

"I'm just…floored." He ran his hands slowly along the top of the steel box in what could only be considered a caress. "I have an E-unit as well, but it's an open system. I have to compress the gas myself, which is tough, and mine's a lot bigger and takes up a ton of space." His gaze landed on me. "Where'd you find it?"

"A few years ago, I was down by the edge of the canals, where the sea crashes into the buildings. They're barely standing anymore." It was a dangerous place to be, unstable and harrowing. "I stumbled onto a floor that held an old manufacturing lab. I had no idea what they used to make. I didn't find much, most of it gone or broken beyond repair. I almost left empty-handed, but as I was exiting, I happened to glance in one more room. There it was. It was too big to carry out in one piece, so I went back three times. I risked my life for this thing." I ran my hand along the top of it, next to Darby's. The E-unit was a meter and a half wide and a meter high. It rested on a raised garden bed. It contained vessels that heated our ample supply of water, and as the H2O steamed, the unit split the hydrogen from the oxygen and pressurized the hydrogen into cubes. Instant vaporized fuel. "Rainwater flows automatically from the roof through that tube." I pointed to the left side of the ceiling. "I use the oxygen it produces for my residence. It runs through that vent."

Darby turned to me, his expression thoughtful. "Holly, I knew you were industrious. I knew you were smart. I knew you were fearless. I knew you had access to goods I could only dream about. But I had no idea what you were doing was as big as this." He gestured to the unit. "This is a game changer."

I slung my arm around Darby shoulders. "Let's head back inside. We've got lots to discuss. I'll tell you more about my tech, and you get to tell me why you were roaming the canals alone at night." I grinned. "In case you were wondering, I haven't forgotten."

Chapter 10

"I didn't catch that last part. Try it again, slower this time, please." We were seated on the bench in front of my screen. "Darby, I'm serious, you have to explain it again in layman's terms. I'm smart and industrious. I can rig up a battery pack. I can install a solar panel. I can reroute plumbing. But I'm not at your level when it comes to bioengineering and human genetics."

We'd been talking awhile, and try as I might, I couldn't get Darby to divulge exactly why he'd been in the canals. But I'd finally managed to get him to talk about some general aspects.

"I can't tell you the location or the person I'm working with," he insisted. "So don't ask, but the government involvement in Plush goes much deeper than you'd think."

I leaned forward, my face set. "What I think is the government has been involved for a very long time. They've been keeping seekers high for years, because honestly, where else would they get their fixes? It's not like we have the recipe for Plush. The government assumes blissed-out seekers are less of a threat than ones in rage-mode—and they're not exactly wrong. But what you just told me is a bigger game changer than my E-unit. Being able to *reverse* the effects of Plush—that's *huge*. I didn't follow along with the genetic cell mutation stuff, or the filling in the breaks of the filaments with bio-matter stuff, but if you can do such a thing, it…I mean, it would change the course of our civilization as we know it. There are upwards of ten thousand seekers inside the city limits alone. That's a fourth of our population." It was impossible to know exactly how many were out there, but the impact of curing them would be incredible. "If you could reverse the damage done to their bodies after years of abuse, this city would be revitalized. Not to mention a ton safer." Death by seeker was a violent affair. It involved a lot of ripping and scratching and biting.

"It would be a game changer, but don't get too ahead of yourself," Darby cautioned. "It's an extreme long shot, as I've said. But the person I'm working with happens to be brilliant, and the engineering is groundbreaking. I think there's a chance. If not full reversal of symptoms, at least partial. It would allow them to function more normally."

"I'm happy to supply you with anything you need." I sat back, my brain ticking through all the massive implications. "Seriously. I have more stuff than anyone knows about. I can be an asset."

"I'll pass that on."

"So, you've been coming to the canals how often and for how long?"

"Twice a week for the last two months," he answered sheepishly. Darby was good at being sheepish. His large eyes fluttered and his cheeks blushed a very cute tint of red. Darby looked like the boy next door—when there had actually been boys next door. I didn't have much to compare it to, but he was boyish and innocent. Everyone loved Darby.

I crossed my arms. "How many seekers have you fought off?"

"None."

My eyebrows rose. "If you've entered this area that many times, the law of averages is not in your favor. I run into a seeker every fifth time." He shrugged, glancing at my battery wall, pretending to be distracted by the large conglomeration of shiny metal discs. "Oh, no, you don't." I play-slugged his arm. "You don't get to go silent on this. How are you getting in and out without issue?"

He sighed, turning back reluctantly. "If I tell you, it could compromise the operation."

I appraised him, taking in his guarded demeanor and serious expression. His brown hair was cut short and had calmed down and dried from its time under his helmet. He'd taken off his protective jacket, and he wore standard-issue clothing provided by the government. A simple long-sleeved shirt in a brown hue, the pants made from a little thicker material, same color. They were uniforms by all accounts. The government didn't have much in the way of imagination. "Okay, I give up. You don't have to tell me. But anything that could help me avoid seekers is good knowledge to have."

He nodded readily. "Oh, I agree. I'll be ready to talk more freely in a month or so." He leaned forward conspiratorially. I met him halfway, our heads almost touching. "Now it's time for you to tell me about the quantum drive and the pico." He nodded toward my sleeping area. "And how you ended up as a sustainer. Honestly, that's the most puzzling piece of the story." When I made a face, he added, "I know you have a heart, Holly. I just always assumed it was more of a murky purple color than gold."

"Are you implying that I'm a coldhearted bitch?" I asked, arching back, making a face that exaggerated a pretend offense. "Because if you are, you'd be correct. I actually have no idea what came over me," I chuckled as I ran a hand through my hair. "I guess he kind of reminded me of myself at that age. And he knows a bunch of stuff I don't." I met Darby's gaze. "There's a new child-slavery ring in town, and this kid was in the middle of it."

Darby whistled low. "Child slavery? That hits close to home. No wonder you took him in."

The crew knew most of my backstory, but they hadn't learned it from me. Bender had told them, with my blessing. It wasn't something I talked about often.

I stood and made my way over to the cooling unit to get more water. The jug was almost empty, so I brought it over to a patch on the wall, slid the piece of metal I had inserted there to the side, and popped the plug. Water gushed inside, filling quickly. When it was full, I covered the spigot back up and poured myself a glass. "You want another cup?" I asked. "I also have some of the amino stuff, but I can't stand it."

"No, I'm good," he answered.

The crisp, white building was on the wall screen now with the blue sky juxtaposed, the lofty billowing clouds floating above it. It would've been a pleasure to see such a sight in real life. I sighed as I sat back down. "Three days after I turned nine," I started, "I killed the leader of the slavery ring who'd taken me captive with my bare hands. With my 'unusual-colored hair' and my 'emergence of breasts,' they were getting ready to sell me to the highest bidder, so I'd had no choice."

"Jesus," Darby whispered. "I'm sorry."

"Don't be," I said, shaking my head as my index finger traced the outer rim of the cup. "I'd refused to cooperate, and I'd been beaten for days. But I got my revenge in the end. Not only did I free myself, but eight others. The man I killed was an animal and had been using the boys as his playthings." I curled my lip at the memory, bile making its way up the back of my throat. I had no idea what happened to the other kids. I'd done the deed, escaped, and never looked back.

As luck would have it, I'd found Bender the next day.

I'd been broken and weary, but alive. If it hadn't been for him, I shudder to think how my life would've ended, because it would've been snuffed out quickly. I'd had no method of survival except my instincts, which were there, but had yet to be honed. My mother had died months before, and she'd sheltered me from our world the best she could, making me dependent and weak, instead of strong and able.

"That's terrible."

Telling Darby wasn't as hard as I'd imagined it would be. "I did the killing with a shard of metal from a broken plank they'd beaten me with, then played dead for a day and a half. It was pure luck that the ringleader came in to dispose of me himself. I jammed the thing into his neck, and that was that." I shrugged.

Darby was wide-eyed. "I can't even imagine. I had both my parents until age nineteen. Daze is lucky to have you."

I smiled. "I only agreed to be his sustainer for one year. After that, he's on his own."

"Yeah, whatever you say."

"I mean it." I stood. "I'm going to teach him everything I know and set him free. He's scrappy, he'll figure it out. It's not like I'll leave him empty-handed. I'll give him the right equipment and make sure he has the survival skills he needs. I'm not a monster." I walked over to a drawer and took out a blanket, setting my cup on the rail. It was old and worn, but it didn't smell even close to as bad as the one in the craft. "All I have to offer you is this bench for sleeping."

"It's more than fine." Darby extended his legs, reclining, his boots hanging over the end. "Where I sleep at home is barely better and certainly doesn't have such an amazing view. It's really something that your screen still works. It defies all logical explanation." I spread the blanket over him. He yawned. "What about the pico? How are you going to find it?"

"I'm taking the kid to Port Station tomorrow. We'll go from there." I hit the lights on the way out, leaving the screen on. "Good night."

"Night."

The first thing on the agenda was to get out of these clothes and into the cleaning stall. Then it was a straight ten hours for me. I needed it.

Before I headed into the waste room, I stopped in front of Daze's unit. There was no movement inside and I couldn't lift the lid without waking him. But I stood beside it, like an anxious mother, my mind drifting to the day I met Bender. I'd been limping, my clothes torn and bloody. Blackout had just begun, the streets dark and foreboding, the rain cold on my exposed skin. I'd had nowhere to go. I'd just killed a man. I'd barely been in my right mind. But I'd known—even at nine years old—that my life was not up for grabs and that I was willing to do anything it took to survive.

Looking back, I had no idea why I'd been so steadfast in my thinking. This world—the one I'd been born into—was the epitome of ruthless and cold. It chewed people up and spit them out on a daily basis. By all reasoning, giving up would've been a hell of a lot easier.

But it'd been impossible for me then, just as it was now. I'd always been a fighter. Every battle I entered, I wanted to win, hands down.

Or die trying.

Chapter 11

The ultraviolet light tingled my skin, the hairs on my arms slowly rising to attention. I stretched as best I could in the confines of the pod, my arms spreading at awkward angles. I managed to get the job done, my muscles protesting the movement.

They'd much prefer I leave them alone and let them sleep.

The heat felt great, warm and gooey, energizing me. It'd been a while since I'd dosed up on vitamin D. It was hard to make it a priority when you were busy trying to survive. Even though I was sore, I felt loose. "Sorry, guys," I told my muscles, my voice cracking with sleep. "It can't be helped. We've got shit to do and people to see." I stretched again, all the way down to my curling toes.

Waking up like this wasn't the worst thing in the world. It was leagues better than fumbling for my Gem because I'd heard a clatter that couldn't be named. I'd even closed the top last night, but only because Darby was sleeping in the other room.

I would've awoken to his screams if anything had gone wrong.

After approximately seven more minutes, my lid cleared and popped open.

Next to me, Daze's did the same.

Before I even sat up, the kid was out of his, hurrying to the waste room. I knew the feeling. "Make sure none of the green splashes on your skin," I called. "If it does, jump into the cleaning stall and turn it on."

Dragging my legs over the side, I poked my toes into the cold room. A shiver raced through me. Now my hair was on end for a different reason. It summed up life in this place perfectly—hot to cold in an instant. Once I was out, I slid open a drawer next to the unit and picked out an identical outfit from yesterday.

I had more clothes than most, having scavenged for them for most of my life. Four years ago, I'd paid a talented seamstress, an acquaintance of Bender's, to cut a bunch of items up and sew together some outfits for me. She had a foolproof method for extracting thread from old clothes to use for new ones. She was worth her weight in coin.

I wasn't used to waiting for my time in the waste room so, clothes in hand, I padded into my living space. Darby was half on, half off the bench, snoring loudly, the blanket crumpled on the floor. I didn't have the heart to wake him yet. Instead, I rested my back against the wall and, like I had hundreds of times before, my eyes slowly tracked the clouds over the mysterious white building with the crisp, clean lines.

It never got old.

The kid emerged from doing his business, and I made my way back.

Daze had his clean clothes and was in the process of sticking a scrawny leg into a pant leg. I yawned as I passed. "Your hair is blond like mine," I told him. "I wasn't expecting that." I walked into the waste room and began to slide the door shut.

The kid grinned. "My mom said my dad had blond hair, too. Maybe he was your brother?"

Any kind of light hair was an anomaly. The races had been thoroughly mixed over the last hundred and fifty years, and the dominant genes were brown and black. "Not a chance," I said. "If I had a brother, I'd know it. Plus, my parents both had jet-black hair. I'm just a freak."

"I am, too," he said. "We can be freaks together."

"Deal."

I was out, fully dressed and ready to go, in four minutes with no choice but to wake Darby so we could start our day. On my way, I opened up my storage locker and took out my vest, reaching in a pocket and pulling out a watch. Timepieces were hard to find. This watch had been crafted sometime in the twenty-first century. It had a digital readout and had been retrofitted with a nano-helium battery. Time pieces had all but become obsolete by the twenty-second century, saved only by collectors, since everyone had access to time by merely asking whatever device they were closest to what time it was.

My timepiece read 7:47 a.m.

We wouldn't be able to take off to Port Station until later tonight. I wanted to time it just right to hit the border at blackout. That would be the safest and most effective way to enter the city.

"Darby, time to wake up." I tapped the bottom of his foot.

He flung himself awake, sputtering as he managed a complicated spin off my bench, landing on the floor in a flurry of arms and legs.

Laughter erupted behind me as the kid walked into the room. I snickered right along with him. "That was really smooth, Darb. What if I'd actually been an intruder?"

"He would've been smoked," Daze answered as he buzzed straight for the cooling unit, taking out a protein cake and the jug of water. He avoided the amino acid drink. It seemed he was getting smarter and smarter.

I was glad the urchin felt comfortable enough to help himself. One less thing to worry about. "Smoked?" I asked. "Are you talking about dead? Because, yes, the lump on the ground would be dead. Do you hear that?" I grinned down at Darby, who was content to lay there, arms spread, eyes closed. "You'd be dead."

Darby extracted himself slowly, his muscles likely much tighter than mine from all the effort he'd put forth last night. "I'm aware of what smoked means."

Darby heaved his way back on the bench, his hands combing through his hair. Behind him, the screen morphed to the one with bees, and the dreaded buzzing filled the room. Daze had commandeered the remote. "It refers to the smoke that used to come out of guns when they were fired, correct?" He glanced at Daze for approval of his theory.

"Nope." The kid punched a button, and the screen morphed to the mountaintop. My personal fave. "It's the smoke that comes from your body after it's been blasted by a laser. Sometimes the person's clothes even catch on fire." His eyes got big, the whites showing all the way around. "But they don't care, because they're already dead." Death was always a fascinating topic.

Darby shook his head. "I've never seen someone with a smoking hole through their body, so I can't confirm or deny. I also don't own a laser gun. But I have seen enough death to last a lifetime, smoking or not." He stood. "Is it okay if I use your cleaning stall?"

"Go right ahead," I replied. "Once we get to Luce, I'm happy to drop you off if you need a ride."

"That's not necessary." Darby walked away, rubbing his muscles. "Just get me as far as where I met you last night, and I'll take it from there."

I cocked my head, thoughtful. "I'm having trouble equating the new improved always-leaves-his-house Darby with the old catatonic one." He ignored me. I called after him, "This is going to take some getting used to!"

"Tell me about it," he mumbled, snapping the door shut.

"You sure you're going to be fine?" I asked for the third time. "I don't like leaving you here alone with only a taser." Even though seekers were usually less active during the day, that didn't mean you wouldn't encounter any.

We stood in front of the safe room where Darby had made his unexpected appearance last night.

Darby shook his head. "I'm fine. Really."

"Okay. If you say so. Hit me on your phone if you have any issues," I told him. "I can turn Luce around and be back here in no time."

"That won't be necessary, but I appreciate it." He turned to Daze. "It was nice to meet you." He stuck out his hand, and the kid shook it. "Make sure you keep her safe. Holly attracts danger like metal fragments to a macro-magnet."

Daze grinned. "That's why her name is Holly Danger. She told me." There was a hint of pride there. But I was certain it would disappear soon enough. Likely after I gave him the first official order he didn't like.

I didn't hug Darby. That's not what we did. Instead, I gave him a two-finger salute off the top of my helmet and turned down the hallway, the kid trailing after me. "Daze, do you need the rope this time? We're coming up on the rafter."

"No," he replied. "I just couldn't see last night. That's the only reason I needed it."

"Ah, is that so?" I stopped in front of the open window where drizzle lashed down a little heavier than it had yesterday. During our travels here, I hadn't detected any more UACs, which had been a bonus. Whoever had been searching for us last night had given up or were looking elsewhere. "It wasn't because we were shimmying over a skinny rafter more than twelve stories up? Seeing the water in the daytime makes it worse, just so you know. Until we lower the grip line, I'd appreciate it if you held on to my back, just to be on the safe side."

"Okay."

I positioned myself on the beam and waited for Daze to scramble up behind me. The kid dutifully gripped the back of my vest as I held the rope above my head, my gloves making the otherwise slippery connection tight. "Twenty-three steps. That's all we need. Count them out loud or count them in your head, it's all the same."

We were almost to the other side, ready to disembark, when a loud crashing sound erupted from inside the building.

Two seconds later, a seeker came into view, rambling down the hallway in front of us.

Then another.

The building had been compromised.

I reached around, clutching Daze in a death grip by the shoulder, and flung him inside. He landed on the floor, his helmet flying off. "Stay down!" I yelled while I sprang over his head, unhooking both my Gem and taser simultaneously. The seeker was closing in quickly, so I brought my boot up and kicked him squarely in the chest.

He was thrown off balance, stumbling back, crashing into the female just behind him. They weren't in full kill-mode, but they were threatening enough, making frantic movements, growling, and talking gibberish. Their skin was unwashed, their scalps missing chunks of hair, and dried blood covered the man's arms and face.

I aimed my twin barrels at them. "If you get up, you're going to go down again and it's going to hurt a lot." Sometimes, if they were just coming down from a fix, a few words could penetrate the cloud. More noise erupted from the hallway. The stairway had to be compromised. It was the only way onto this floor. "Dammit!" I shouted. Being caught unaware was a pain in the ass. Lockland should have warned me.

My tech phone went off in my vest.

Too late.

The man began to claw his way up off the floor. I had no choice but to tase him. I sent out a charge, and he arced backward, clutching his chest before he went limp, pinning the female.

I made the only decision I had left to make. "We're heading in there," I shouted at Daze, gesturing to a door on the right. I ran, scooting the kid through ahead of me. It wasn't a safe room, per se, but it was a way out. I slammed the door and engaged the bolt Lockland had installed. There was one on every door of this hallway for this very reason.

"Why don't we just go back over the beam?" Daze cried, fear causing his words to quake. "To the building we just came from? There were no seekers there."

"There's no other way to cross into this building from that side, and Luce is in the basement. It would take us all day to circle around the canals to get back here." I holstered my guns, formulating a plan in my head. "If we can't make it out this way, we'll do that, but this building has multiple escape routes. What is this? Lesson number six or seven? Always know your environment." Fists began to hammer on the bolted door. Garbled words like *need* and *Plush* made their way through the gaps.

I walked over and pounded my own hands against it, the sound echoing into the room.

"Why are you doing that?" Daze asked, panicked.

"I'm making as much noise as possible. I want to draw them all to this location. We need the stairwell clear." I positioned my mouth over the seam. "I have your fix of Plush right here. Come and get it!"

As the pounding grew louder from the other side, I wheeled Daze around, guiding him to the back corner. Once there, I cleared some debris out of the way and pried up a floor tile.

A welcoming hole gaped at us from below.

I lay on my stomach, sticking my head down into it, trying to filter out the noise the seekers were making from anything coming from below. After a moment, satisfied, I sat up. "It's a four-meter drop. I know you can do it. It's clear down there. I'll lower you down as far as I can before I let go." I stood, brushing myself off.

"But…but, I don't understand." Daze backed up instead of moving toward the hole. "Why don't you just kill them? You have a Gem." He raised his small hand and pointed to the bottom of my vest. "One laser blast and they don't get back up again."

I took my helmet off so Daze could see my face as I leaned over, settling a hand on his shoulder. "I don't kill indiscriminately. Ever. I only kill if there's no option left. That's rule number eight. It's an important one. Don't forget it. Why do you think we take the time to secure these routes in the first place?" I slid my hand down, hooking it under his elbow, walking him to the front of the hole. "They are human beings who made a stupid choice a long time ago. A debt they are paying for the rest of their lives." Hopefully, that would change if Darby had any say. "Now sit down and let me lower you in. I'll be two seconds behind you."

Chapter 12

The stairway was blissfully empty. The commotion on twelve had drawn all available seekers looking for a fix to that location. I'd hustled Daze down the rest of the flights double time, relieved to see Luce sitting pretty, like nothing harrowing was happening upstairs.

"Get in," I instructed, nodding toward the craft while pulling a tech phone out of my vest. "Jerry, it's Ella," I said into the speaker. "Are we still on for lunch at eleven?"

Two beats later, "Yes, unless you still need help with your sewage problem?" Brief static, then, "I can be over in fifteen."

"Nope," I responded. "It's taken care of. But I could use your help with my cooling unit this afternoon. It's on the fritz."

Lockland was offering to come to my aid, and I told him I was fine, but he'd have a mess to clean up later.

"Will do," he said.

"Instead of meeting on seventh, let's meet on ninth."

"Got it. See you there."

I stowed my phone and pulled out my watch. It'd taken us a little under two hours to get here. It was ten after ten. We were now meeting at Bender's, but I could get there in forty-five minutes, no problem.

Opening Luce's door, I climbed in and punched her starter button. The props engaged immediately as the landing gear retracted. She hovered a meter above the ground.

I patted her dashboard, because I was superstitious like that.

Then I reached in the back, straining, my hips twisting, until I found what I was looking for, my fingers curling around another helmet. I tugged it forward and handed it to Daze, since he'd lost his during the fracas. "Here, put this on. It's going to be as big as the last one, but it'll have to do. I need you covered at all times when we're out in the city until we solve your…issue." I raised an eyebrow. What else were we supposed to call it? "This one doesn't have a full face mask, so you should be able to breathe just fine."

I flipped a lever on the dash, and the wall behind us began to open. I was happy to see that Daze had already, smartly, utilized the shoulder harness as I redirected Luce around in the small space. Turning a gyroless dronecraft in a confined area was trickier than in the wide open, as the props created all sorts of funky wind shear. It was a good thing I'd done this hundreds of times before.

In this exact same spot.

Daze peered into the darkness in front of us. "That's so cool. Are we going inside the building?"

"Yep." I eased the craft forward, punching the lever again once we passed over the line to resecure the room. "This was something called a parking garage before flying became all the rage and, for the most part, people began to park in open-air lots."

Daze fiddled with his harness straps, his voice dropping barely above a whisper. "I'm sorry…for back there." His apology had been uttered almost inaudibly. If I hadn't been concentrating, I would've missed it.

I angled Luce between the columns, making my way up and out. "Don't get in the habit of apologizing for things you had no clue about. But always apologize for rules you knowingly break. Those are words to live by, spoken to me by a very smart man—and one you're about to meet," I said. "Seekers are dangerous, they attack us, and we kill them. It makes sense. I didn't lay everything out for you, so don't worry about it."

"I've never seen one that close before," he said. "I got scared."

We were at the top of the ramp. I slowed the craft to an idle in front of a large door. This one was worn with age, and the internal graphene honeycomb pattern had worn through. I turned to the kid, my arm flexed along the back of his seat. "I was scared, too. I hate surprises. Always have. My friends and I have safeguards in place for that very reason. They should've worked to prevent what happened today. It's been a long time since I've been ambushed. Back in the day, I might've even used my Gem gun." I grinned. "But I'm older and smarter now." I tapped the side of my helmet where my temple was. "I know seekers aren't intentionally trying to harm me. They are fueled by something compulsory we can't understand. Think about it. The same people clawing at that door to try to get to us would've ignored us if they'd been blissed-out on a fresh hit of Plush." We were waiting for the light to blink on the wall. Lockland must be being extra careful. He'd flash it when the street was totally clear. "Now, an outskirt aggressively pointing a laser at my chest? That would be a different story. If someone has intent to harm me, I harm back, and I try to be first. Because if I'm not first, I'm dead."

Daze looked skeptical, his hands dropping to his lap. "You were scared? You didn't seem like it."

"Of course I was. If I hadn't been, how do you think I could've jumped over your head that fast? Did you see that move? If you didn't know me, you'd have thought my legs had enhancements. Fear amps your body, giving you exactly what you need to accomplish your goals. Without it, you're sunk." The light on the wall flicked to green. I punched a button on Luce's dash, and the door began to slide. "I need you to crouch down in your seat. You don't have to go as far under as you did before, but I want your head below the windows."

Daze complied, slouching down in his seat, the harness no match for his bony body. Even at its most cinched, the kid had room to move. "Where are we going?" His new helmet slid down to cover his eyes. He pushed it back, irritated.

"We're heading to Bender's shop. He's a mechanic who can fix anything and everything. Lockland is meeting us there. They're my crew, and they're going to help us formulate a plan to break into your old house tonight. Breaking and entering is kind of my specialty. How does that sound for a fun evening out?"

"Fine, I guess." His listless reply surprised me.

When the wall had fully expanded, I eased Luce out on to the street. "What gives? Last night you were happy about the plans." I lofted us higher immediately. There weren't many rules to operating a dronecraft. The only one anyone followed to the letter was height. Head-on collisions were messy, and no one wanted to crash if they could help it. If you were heading north, you cruised around twenty meters high; south, fifteen; east, ten; west, five. Any lower than five, and you could run into trouble with debris and crap in the lanes.

"Nothing gives," Daze answered. "We can go."

I gained full altitude, no other crafts in sight, my eyes automatically tracking the skies for a matte black Q7. I'd seen him yesterday, but he hadn't seen me. The advantage was all mine, just the way I liked it. My windshield was clear, even though rain pelted down at a steady pace. The surface of the glass was structured so nothing stuck to it. Instead, it beaded and rolled up and over the roof.

I cruised past a series of dilapidated buildings. The city was divided into four quadrants: the canals, Government Square, The North, and The Middle, which was where we were heading. Most law-abiding citizens congregated in the government hub, as it was the most protected. The North was occupied by outskirt types—folks who, for the most part, opposed most laws and chose to live a rougher existence. The North was also home to rathskellers, skells for short. They were some of the only communal gathering spots in the entire city. But these weren't warm and inviting hangouts. They were hostile, edgy establishments where people came together to make deals and trades, gamble, fight, exchange information, and blow off steam. Lots and lots of steam.

I wasn't a fan. If a client hired me to locate something and requested we meet at a skell, I agreed. Always with my Gem in plain sight. I didn't ever choose to frequent them on my own.

The Middle, where Bender lived, was its own protected community. They didn't appreciate outsiders and guarded its borders with gusto. They were a little friendlier than Northerners, but not by much. They also followed the laws, kind of.

I maneuvered around a particularly large outcropping of twisted metal girders, a building that had fallen on its side. "You know, this Tandor guy isn't going to win. I meant what I said yesterday about being your sustainer. It means I keep you alive, which I intend to do."

"You haven't met him yet," Daze countered. "He's the kind of guy that smokes someone just because they disagree with him. You don't even have to be a seeker, you can just be regular."

I met the kid's eyes. They were a mix of amber and brown. Now I understood. "Daze, just because I didn't kill those seekers doesn't mean I won't do what's necessary. You can trust me on that." Three buildings up, I angled left, heading west, dropping altitude quickly, my hands working the levers almost without thought. "Should we pay that sustainer family a visit?" I grinned. "The ones who considered selling you into slavery, and teach them a thing or two?"

His eyes brightened, then dimmed just as quickly. "No. They had another kid. One they took in as a baby."

"Got it." The rules of the street: Protect your own kind. "I'm not anticipating any issues, just so you know." I slowed the craft. Up ahead was the only logjam in the city. "We go in, uncover the goods, and get out. Procuring that pico is incredibly important. Without it, we don't know what we have on this guy." I idled at an intersection where four buildings stood, one on each corner. Visibility was always tough here. One craft flew above us. It was white, not black.

After I was sure it was safe, I continued on.

Only a few more kilometers left to go.

"What if the pico is gone?" Daze asked.

I shrugged. "You said you hid your things well when you left, but if it's not there, it's not there. Life keeps going." A few blocks down, I turned, heading north again, hugging the far right while I increased altitude. "We'll figure out something else. A guy involved with child slavery has dirty hands." After a few minutes, and another turn, I made a quick drop, punching the landing gear as I went. We settled smoothly on top of a building that had been sheared off at three stories. Once we were down, I depressed a button twice, a retractable cover closing over us. I tugged off my helmet. "Now it's time for me and you to meet some of my friends. And don't worry too much. Bender's a badass, but he won't hurt you. He'll just act like he will."

Chapter 13

Bender was the only occupant of the entire building, so it was always secure. There were only two ways in. One up top, where we currently were, and one door at street level that led into his shop—and when that door was closed, it would take more power than the government had to blow it up.

Daze trailed after me, his helmet braced under one arm, like I held mine. Except, his arms were much shorter and the helmet adult-sized, so it looked comical as his hand struggled to keep it in place.

Endearing, but comical.

I headed toward a barricade of solid steel and drew a small laser out of my vest, aiming it into a hole. A light flashed, and a door popped open at the end of the wall.

"Is that a laser key?" Daze asked as we walked toward the entrance.

"Yep," I answered as I widened the span of the opening with my foot so he could move through. "But it's a heat-sensor laser, not a flesh-singeing one. Lesson number nine or ten, not all lasers are created equal." We headed down the first of three flights of stairs. "Bender looks like he should run a skell in The North," I warned, "and quite possibly used to. He doesn't talk about his past, so don't get any ideas about asking him."

"We're in The Middle, aren't we?" Daze asked.

"Yep."

"Me and my friends tried to get in here a couple times." He trailed a few paces behind me. "Once we were successful, but got tossed a few minutes later. One guy got a broken arm."

"That's what happens around here. They don't take kindly to strangers," I said. "If they let one orphan in, the floodgates would open to them all. Everyone here is hanging on by a thread, exactly like the rest of us. They're just doing it more united than most. They let you in to see Bender if you ask nicely and have something in need of repair, but you have to request a visit ahead of time. No sneaking in. Other than that, their motto is: Stay Out."

"Is that how you met Bender?" Daze asked. "Did you need something fixed?"

"Not exactly." We rounded the last landing, another steel door in front of us. No fancy apparatuses to get through this one. It could be opened only from the inside. I took out my tech phone, but before I could depress the button, the door swung wide, ending on a loud creak.

Just inside, Bender had his back against the wall, his massive arms crossed, a pissed expression on his face. He wore a tan one-piece outfit, the kind government workers used when they "worked" on city projects. *Work* was a bit of an oxymoron. The government came out reluctantly and did things, but only when the situation was dire and lives had already been lost. The sleeves were cut off right above his biceps. Otherwise, the thing wouldn't have fit.

I prodded Daze forward, my hand resting beneath his shoulder blades, urging him through the opening. His feet scuffed in his unconscious resistance. It would've been nice if Bender could've found a smile for the kid, but that wasn't how this was going to work.

Instead, Bender's cleanly shaved head, deeply veined arms, and pierced ears—all meant to intimidate—were doing their job perfectly. Everyone in The Middle feared and respected Bender in equal parts, and now that included the kid.

How else did the man have an entire building to himself?

"This is Daze, my sustainee." My voice issued a minor challenge, even though I knew it wasn't necessary. My business was my business. "I picked him up last night. Sorry I didn't signal it. That was my fault all the way." After we were both inside, the door shut automatically. "Darby was in the area, so it all worked out."

Bender focused his attention on the kid, who bumped back into me trying to get away from his jet-black stare.

I placed a hand on Daze's shoulder so he knew I was there. I could sympathize. The first time I'd seen Bender, I'd wet my pants. It was only a trickle, but still, there had been urine involved. I'd been nine, fresh from escaping the horror of a man who I'd killed and looked way less scary than Bender.

Daze was twelve. He'd likely fare better. But I was here just in case.

Bender's eyes tracked back to mine. "Is this the kid you were hired to find last night?"

"Yep."

Without saying another word, Bender turned and lumbered down the hallway.

We followed, me gently kneeing Daze in the back to get him started. I leaned over his shoulder as we walked. "Lesson eleven, never show them you're scared." Daze's spine straightened immediately. That's the spirit, kid.

Bender's workshop was massive. Once upon a time, it'd been a retail space of some sort. The glass in front had been replaced with thick graphene walls. Pillars were positioned at regular intervals, keeping everything standing, and the mezzanine floor, which had likely been polished to a high sheen long ago, was marred by the passing of time and pocked with holes made from dropping large, heavy items on it on a regular basis.

Bender had worktables, spread with parts, motors, rotors, tools, and everything else, scattered all over the place. Nothing looked organized. It never had been. Yet, of course, Bender knew where everything was. He also had traps and weapons stashed at two-meter intervals, so you had to know where to step. Even though he was feared in this neighborhood, it didn't make him immune to issues. There were always issues.

I laid my helmet on a pile of bolts and carefully took Daze's out of his arms. The kid was too overcome to talk. "Looks like we beat Lockland here," I said as I glanced around.

Bender sat on his usual stool, one foot up on a rung, his arms back to being crossed. "What happened on twelve today?"

I slid a chair out and sat. "We were overrun. Had no warning. Came over the rafter from Blue into Yazzie, and there they were. Tased one, he collapsed on the other, and me and the kid dropped through a ceiling hole. Stairs were clear by the time we got there, the garage was open, and here we are." Hollow pounding came from the hallway we'd just come through. Lockland was at the door. I nodded casually. "You want me to get that?"

Bender flicked his head. "Send the kid."

My eyebrows rose, but I didn't question it. I turned to Daze. "Go answer the door. The guy standing there is a little shorter and a little nicer-looking than this guy"—I jerked my thumb toward Bender—"but not by much. There's a red button and a green button. Hit the red one. If you hit the green, you'll wish you hadn't for about a week." It took Daze only two seconds to react.

I would've given him a solid ten. He buzzed back the way we'd come, no questions asked.

I focused my attention on Bender.

He gave an infinitesimal nod.

His way of saying he approved. I left it alone.

Daze and Lockland entered thirty seconds later. Lockland was wearing his usual jacket, a long sweeping black synthetic leather throwback. I'd salvaged it a few years ago. It'd had Lockland written all over it. Where Bender was bald, Lockland wore his dark hair clipped close to the scalp. Lockland's coloring leaned more toward mocha. Bender's was light brown. They both looked rough as hell, facial hair usually shadowing their jaws, scars and other life lessons embedded on their skin for all to see. When they walked the streets, regular folks took a step back.

My family.

"What the fuck, Holly?"

"What the fuck yourself, Lockland? We were overrun. Why in the hell didn't we have any warning?"

"The sensors were down in Yazzie on twelve, but I didn't know it until I lost track of you halfway over the rafter. When I figured out something was off, I beeped." Lockland swept himself into a chair, while Daze lingered behind me.

"Your beep came too late. Seekers were all over. I'm assuming you saw where we went after? Or was all of Yazzie down?"

He shook his head. "Just twelve and the stairwell. I

picked you up on eleven, then again in the garage. The bigger question is, who the hell is after you and why? That shit was deliberate. Whoever it is can dismantle a signal amplifier quickly, and they knew what to look for." Lockland reclined back, his chair banging against a worktable. He ignored things as they tumbled off.

"They aren't after me," I said. "Well, they are now, but I wasn't their initial quarry." I inclined my head toward the kid, who had come to stand next to me. "You tell them the rest. All of it."

Both men turned their attention to Daze.

Back in the day, I might've wilted under such scrutiny, but the urchin stuck his now clean chin out. It seemed he'd recovered from his first sight of Bender. But, of course, Bender was sitting a few meters away, trying to look smaller than he was. I appreciated that. "I…I took something of Tandor's…and he's going to kill me for it," the kid started. "But Holly said if I can find the computer, maybe we can get him to stop." He paused. When nobody said anything, he continued. "Tandor is new in town and a bad man. I'm a runaway…from Port Station. I came here…to the city…after my mom died. I got snatched. A bunch of us were hiding in the tunnels, and they came for us. Tandor threatened to kill my friend, so I took a chip out of his computer." His chin jutted even farther. Impressive angle. "I knew where to find it because my dad had a pico. The chip is called a quantum drive. Tandor bragged to his friend that nobody could figure out how to get the drive. But I did."

Lockland's head dropped back, and Bender massaged the knuckles on one hand.

The kid had no idea how high the stakes were. If my family chose to protect the kid, they took on all his baggage.

I stood, my hands dropping to my waist, my gloved fingers flexing. "I made the decision to help the kid. It's mine alone. The two of us are heading to Port Station tonight. It's my run. It's not universal. Once we get the computer, then I'll have more information to share. Until then, I'm in this alone." I was giving them a chance to stay out of a potential maelstrom. They'd do the same for me.

"Bullshit." Lockland stood abruptly. The table rocked precariously as he strode away, more crap tumbling off. "This Tandor asshole wrecked my equipment. Someone has to pay for that."

Without comment, Bender stood and walked over to his cooling unit and took out a jug containing a sludgy brown liquid. He popped the cap and downed it straight from the bottle. Not everyone hated aminos. A knock came from his front door. He swiped a forearm over his mouth and roared, "I'm closed. Come back later!" Then he shoved the jug back in the unit, not offering it to anyone else, and came to stand in front of Daze and me, arms crossed. It was his standard pose—the same exact one I'd encountered eighteen years ago when I'd stumbled through his front door trying to outrun the neighborhood militants. "This run is universal."

That was it.

"Got it." I nodded. "After we see what's on the quantum drive, I don't care what happens to the pico. Darby wants to take a look at it, though. We can vote later. My plan is to hit Port Station at the beginning of blackout. Daze has a good memory, and he's going to draw us a map. His place was fairly run-down when he left, so we're assuming it's resident-free. If not, I'll deal."

Bender eyed Daze. "Who else knows you came from Port Station?"

Daze gaped at the direct question.

If I had resting bitch voice, Bender had a punch-you-in-the-neck voice, usually followed up by a growl. Before the kid had a chance to answer, Lockland interjected, coming forward, "What he means is, did you talk to the other street kids? Did you brag? Who knows about your stuff?" Lockland's tone wasn't much better, but it conveyed its true meaning, which was *I'll slap you upside the head if you don't answer quickly.*

Daze was ready this time. "I told a few people. I didn't brag. I just talked about my mom."

"Did you tell them exactly where you lived? The address? If you told anyone, Tandor and his crew will find out eventually."

"I only told Renata. My best friend. But she's dead."

"The one you tried to save?" I asked.

"Yes." Daze scuffed his shoes on the ground.

There was no way to know if Renata talked before she died. "There's a silicon tablet and static pen over there. Go draw us a picture of your residence and anything else you can remember around it. I've been to Port Station enough times. It's not that big. I should be able to pick out some familiar landmarks."

"Where were you supposed to drop this kid yesterday?" Bender asked as Daze went to do as I asked.

"In The North," I said. "The address is on a stencil inside my craft. The job came through a communication slot I monitor outside of the canals. I haven't been back to that location."

Lockland paced forward, scowling, sidestepping a trap at the last minute that would've plowed the tip of a pointed hammer into his thigh. "They know something about you. They went to Yazzie to track you down, which means they were following you." As he paced, his jacket kicked out behind him. He didn't wear standard-issue clothing. Lockland's number-one job was security, but he'd started out as a salvager, just like me.

"Could be," I said, "but Luce didn't pick up any craft signals on the way back, and there's no way anyone compromised her while we were in transit. She wasn't out of my sight. The only thing solid I have so far is that they operate a matte black Q7. Luce scrambled her up no problem, so their tech can't be that advanced. It didn't trail us home."

"Knowing anything about you makes them dangerous." Lockland tugged a chair out and straddled it backward, facing us. "From now on, we only take level-three avenues, no more level ones until we figure their angle." Level threes were basically tunnels and routes we hadn't used in years. It would make getting anywhere much harder, but it would keep us under the radar.

"Somebody's got to tell Darby," I said. "I'd bet money he doesn't remember any of our level threes, and he's been out more often lately." I wasn't going to rat out his business. It was his story to tell.

"Stay out of your main residence, too," Bender growled. "If they know about Yazzie, they know more." He fisted his hands, bracing his knuckles on one of his tables, leaning over, bowing his head. This was how Bender used his brain best. After a moment, he lifted it and said, "I don't like it. Something's off. If there are new outskirts in town, we should've heard about it. This is my town." His eyes locked on Daze. "When did you get snatched?"

"Two months ago," Daze answered promptly, his voice a few octaves higher. "I know that for sure, because the other kids gave me my six-month cake the day before."

"Cake?" I asked.

"A protein cake," he answered. "For surviving that long. It was supposed to be chocolate flavored." He shrugged. "It tasted like normal."

Chapter 14

"Does any of this look familiar?" I asked.

"I can't see, it's dark out," Daze answered from the passenger seat sullenly.

"Look harder." We hovered over one of the walls on the east side of Port Station. The guards were spread out along this stretch, and easily bribed, which Lockland had seen to during the day.

Lucky for us, Daze lived close to this area. The buildings, just beyond the wall, were much different than they were in the city, most of them low and crumbling, made from materials not meant to last. This had been a neglected area, even before the dark days, most of the buildings slated for removal rather than upgrades.

Daze squashed his head against the windshield, his helmet sliding back as it hit the glass. He had my spare glasses on for better viewing. Bender had given him new headgear, but it still wasn't small enough.

While I waited for him to recognize the landscape, my tech phone buzzed. It was already in my hand. "This is Ella."

"You're late for dinner." Lockland was irritated. During the day, he'd discovered that more of his equipment had been vandalized in a few other buildings we used in the canals. Whoever had been searching for us last night had done a fairly thorough job and seemed to know the routes we used, which was alarming for a variety of reasons.

This was why you kept your residences a secret. The fewer people who knew your movements, the better off you were.

"I know. We're running late." I let go of the button, then depressed it again. "Waiting for Rennie to arrive." Lockland had let Daze pick his handle. The kid had gone for a shout-out to his lost pal. It'd made my heart do that clenchy thing again. I let go of the button and turned to Daze. "Lockland's antsy, and we don't want that. We need to land this thing. Does anything seem familiar? It should. According to your map, we're right on top of things."

"It's darker out than it was yesterday," Daze countered. That was true. Sometimes the cloud cover was thicker, allowing less of the moon to filter through.

I made an executive decision. I depressed the button one more time and said, "Heading over now. Remember, Rennie likes his cake warm." I stuck my phone in a front pocket, easily accessible, and eased Luce forward. If Daze thought it was hard to see, try operating a craft in the dark with no headlamps. It was a good thing my eyes were used to seeing little to guide me.

I'd been in this part of Port Station only twice before, but I knew there was an open space on top of a gnarled old building right over the wall. I just had to find it. Unfortunately, we didn't have set routes in Port Station. It was too small. Roughly three square kilometers. But today, between the four of us, we'd been able to come up with a fairly solid plan.

Static came through my phone, and a second later, Bender's voice came through my vest pocket. "I'm not gonna be able to make it tonight. Enjoy your meal without me."

I had both hands on the controls. "Shit."

Daze recognized the alarm in my voice. "What?"

"Lockland bribed the guards on the way in, but Bender just let us know that the way out was going to be trickier. Either somebody backed out, or they couldn't make contact with the next shift." I began to lower Luce onto what I hoped was the right location, engaging her landing gear. I could make out a silhouette of an old fan unit beneath us, so it looked about right.

We were going to find out in about ten seconds.

Luce's right side hit first, and as I tried to steady her, the left side came down a meter lower with a large clunk. I'd found the fan, but instead of landing next to it, I'd landed on it. Once the craft settled, I punched her off. "This is going to have to do. We can't afford the noise or time to go up and try again. I've parked here before. Last time, the building was abandoned." We didn't have to worry about seekers either. Port Station was small, and they were able to deal with them.

Departing the craft at a serious angle was going to be interesting. My door scraped the roof as it lifted, and I made my way out as gracefully as I could— which hadn't been anywhere near graceful, it was a mess of contortions and shimmying and trying to exhale myself thinner. Finally on the outside, I beckoned Daze to slide out my side, since his was up in the air. He unbuckled and scooted toward me. He exited just fine. The advantages of a small frame.

The basics of the plan were: He would lead me to his old house, hide outside while I went in, I would get the stuff, and then we would get the hell out.

I shut the door once Daze was out, and we made our way to the edge of the building at a crouch. "Anything look familiar now?" I whispered.

"I'm not sure."

Not exactly the help I was hoping for.

"According to your map, we're only a few blocks away. The buildings around here are low, so we've got a good vantage point from up here. You said your place was next to one of the taller buildings." I scanned the horizon in front of us. "How about that one?" I gestured to one that looked like it fit the description.

"Yeah, that looks like it."

That was good enough for me.

Instead of going into the building via the door and risking encountering anyone, I headed to the other side to an old fire escape. It was rusted, slightly misshapen, and missing sections, but it would accomplish the goal of getting us closer to the ground.

I glanced over the edge, relieved to see it was still there.

"Same routine as last time," I told Daze. "I lean over and drop you down, and then I come after." He nodded as he sat on the edge. I braced my waist against the lip, linking my arm around his, bending over as far as I could. "Ready?"

"Ready."

I let go.

He landed with his legs compressed, tottering a bit as he tried to catch his balance. I held my breath. Half of the guard rail was missing. He finally stood, glancing up at me and giving me a thumbs-up.

I lowered myself off the side, the front of my vest scraping against the surface of the rough bricks, my gloves keeping my grip solid for the umpteenth time in their lives. Man, I loved these gloves. "Head down the steps. I'll be right behind you." I let go once he moved, dropping to the platform. The weight of my landing caused the entire structure to quake and wobble. I grabbed on to a portion of the remaining rail to steady myself. Daze was already two flights down, and I hurried to catch up.

We both made it to the bottom without issue. I set my finger against my lips, gesturing for him to follow quietly. We kept low to the ground, that being easier for the kid than me, but I had this hunched-while-running thing down pat. I was surprised my back wasn't permanently curved after all these years of trying to keep out of sight.

A noise came from up ahead, and I veered us in between two buildings, tugging Daze along. Just because it was blackout, didn't mean people stopped moving around. Port Station was safer than the city as far as seekers went, but worse for everyday petty crime. There were too few resources to go around. It made people edgy.

A few minutes later, two bodies moved past our location.

We'd taken cover behind a pile of building scraps. Their silhouettes suggested that they were male, but they didn't speak, so it was hard to know. I counted to sixty before I eased us out onto the road. The men had already turned off our street. I leaned over to Daze, whispering in his ear, "We're going to cross here. We stick to the shadows. Two blocks up, we take a left, then a right, and we should arrive at your residence."

Daze was smart not to reply.

I took off, the kid following less than a meter behind. I enjoyed that I didn't have to keep reiterating my rules. It made things easier and I was fond of easier.

Once we were within a block, I drew my Gem and my taser. I carried my Gem in my right hand, my taser in my left. Daze knew the plan. He'd told me where he hid the pico—under some old stair treads behind a door in his bedroom that led to an unused attic space that had been walled off long ago. In front of his building, I elbowed him in the shoulder to make sure we were in the right place.

He glanced up and nodded.

I searched for an adequate hiding place to stow him. A large abandoned trash bin sat a few meters away. It was piled high, likely containing years old refuse, making a good blockade. I led Daze over, gesturing for him to scoot behind it. "Stay put," I whispered on the barest breath. "I'm going to circle the perimeter just to make sure before I go in. It doesn't look like anybody occupies this place, so that's good."

Daze nodded.

Before I went to investigate, I withdrew my tech phone and pressed the button twice, letting Bender and Lockland know I was ready to enter. If they didn't hear from me within a half hour, they'd back me up. Lockland was positioned outside the regular city limits, waiting to see what happened. Then I put on my chromes.

Creeping stealthily around the building, I stopped at intervals to listen, my shoulder brushing against the chipped stone, my feet sidestepping the inevitable trash. I heard nothing, not even people in nearby homes. This must be a less-desirable neighborhood in Port Station, which was fine by me. At the main entrance, I ducked inside, crossing the threshold where a door should've been.

Daze had said his residence was on the third floor. This entire building was only three stories high and held six units. Dodging several piles of debris, my weapons up, my arms sweeping back and forth, I came to a stop at the base of the stairway. Still no noise, which meant this might end up being a peaceful transaction. If we'd made it here before Tandor decided to try and track down Daze to get his quantum drive back, we were golden.

Carefully picking my way up to the third floor, I stopped midclimb, cocking my head. I wasn't sure if I'd heard a noise or not. The sound had been so low it could've been anything, including a tap of rain on the roof.

I stayed still for a full minute.

The sound did not repeat itself.

I had two options. I could continue, or I could retreat. If I retreated, we ran the risk of not being able to capture our booty. If the noise had been nothing, the trip would be a waste.

The prize was too great and I continued.

My foot tentatively tracked up to the next tread, my back against the wall, my weapons aimed in either direction. The Gem was deadly, and the taser would incapacitate for at least an hour.

The hallway at the top was short. Daze had said his unit was on the left. I pivoted, crossing the landing, my head swiveling. I brought my taser hand up to my glasses and clicked through the dials. No heat signatures, no ultraviolet, and no gammas, which meant the area I was inspecting was clear of people and anything transmitting a signal, which could be a variety of tech items and bombs.

I eased open the door of Daze's unit, wincing at the squeak, placing my back against the wall inside, crouching down low to the floor, listening. As I gazed around the dim space, my heart broke a little. It appeared his mother had tried her best, but the room was filled with broken furniture and discarded items. Things had fallen onto the floor and hadn't been picked up again. In the corner sat a ratty mattress, the blankets old and shredded. Various clothing items lay scattered around. Daze had said that his mother had slept out here and had given him the only private sleeping area.

Easing up, I made my way toward the back of the unit, entering a short hallway. A waste room sat to my right, open windows to my left. My target was straight ahead. The waste room door was ajar enough for me to get a glimpse inside. It held a sad-looking chem-toilet and a space to stand over a drain for cleaning.

Continuing on, I stopped at the entry of Daze's room, leaning my head inside. I scanned the area. There were two doors across the short expanse, one on the far left and one on the right. According to Daze, one was to a closet, and one led to a set of stairs to an old attic space.

The closet door, to the left, was cracked open. The one on the right was closed. That was the one I needed. Daze said he'd hidden the computer and some valuables under one of the treads. I'd promised to get everything he'd left. Unlike the outer room, Daze's area was completely free of junk. The mattress, although old and filthy, had a blanket folded at the end. There was a picture on the wall—a painting of some kind that had faded beyond recognition. Nothing in the room was integrated like my place in the canals. Instead, a small table with a single drawer sat next to his mattress.

With my Gem gun aimed in front of me, I made my way to the closed door.

In and out.

I holstered my taser and grasped the knob, right as a noise erupted from behind. I swung my arm around, my body trying to follow, but my movement was impeded by a large hand cupping my mouth tightly, hot breath on my neck. "If you want to save the kid, don't make a sound."

Chapter 15

Making a sound wasn't my intention, but breaking out of the iron grasp holding me was. My shoulder shot backward, using my attacker as a counterweight, aided by my legs, with enough force to make the man gasp.

I was well versed in hand-to-hand combat and had been since the age of ten. When Bender was your sparring partner as a kid, you learned a thing or two.

Instead of letting me go, the man dragged me backward, forcing me into the closet where he'd obviously been lying in wait. I swore, the hand still over my lips muzzling the sound, for not checking it first. He must've positioned himself behind the door so I didn't pick up on his heat signature.

I was going to pay dearly for that mistake.

"I'm not going to hurt you," he hissed as I brought my heel up, crashing it into his knee. He buckled, but didn't lose his grip. He had to be as big as Bender, judging by the barrel of the chest I currently pressed up against, along with the height of his shoulders, which were above mine. "They've already been here."

I stopped struggling for a moment.

"If you want to save the kid, who you stashed outside, do as I say." The timbre of his voice was deep and raspy, his words gritty. There was no doubt in my mind that he was an outskirt. He smelled like one, too, musky with a lingering scent of liquid fuel.

My Gem gun was still out, but he had that arm in a firm grasp, his grip painful as his fingers dug into my flesh. I wasn't about to give up. I rotated my upper torso as much as I could, angling my head forward, then twisted my body, bashing my head back with as much momentum as I could garner from my locked position.

I connected solidly with his face.

He let go, bracing both of his hands over his gushing nose, which I'd just broken with a satisfying crack.

I pivoted, both hands gripping the handle of my gun, aiming it at his neck. The only part of him exposed. It would do.

He dropped his hands and held them out in front of him, blood continuing to pour from both nostrils. Through my infrared glasses, it looked odd, like two pools of rapidly moving heat.

"We both want the same thing," he ground out, his words edgy.

"I highly doubt that." My voice was like ice. I'd been

taken by surprise two times today, twice too fucking many.

"I've been tracking you." I couldn't see his features. They were covered by a helmet and a visor, and he wore a long trench coat and dark underclothes. But I was one hundred percent certain he wasn't familiar to me. I'd remember that voice anywhere. I didn't respond. Instead, I tapped a finger on the trigger. He continued, "I saw you with the boy. By the cliff. I'm looking for Tandor. We want the same thing."

"Keep talking."

He shrugged, his hands still up, his nose releasing blood. It must be a bad break. "That's it."

"How did you know how to find the boy by the gorge?" I asked.

"I have someone on the inside."

A scream rent the air.

It was high pitched, followed by frantic yelling. Daze. I turned to race out of the closet, but was caught by the elbow. I used the twisting motion in my favor as my attacker yanked me backward. My fist rose automatically, connecting with his neck as I spun.

He sputtered as he fell backward, but he didn't loosen his grip on my arm.

Dammit.

I brought my leg up to kick him where it would hurt the most, but he pivoted out of the way, all while hauling me up against him. My free hand gripped his upper arm. It was unyielding.

Blood covered the bottom half of his face like an oil slick, including his teeth as he flashed them centimeters from mine. "Listen to me, goddammit," he snarled. "They're taking the kid, and there's nothing you can do about it. There are too many, and they have weapons they're not afraid to use—bombs that could blow up this entire town."

I struggled to break free, but he held firm. I tilted my head back as a primal roar issued out of my throat. "Let me go!"

Noise sounded inside the building.

Feet tracking upward.

Before I knew it, the mystery man with the iron grip whipped me around in the small space and shoved me through a trapdoor in the floor. I landed on my feet in the unit below and wasted no time making my exit. I raced into the bedroom. Behind me, there was a loud thump as the man came down after me, his heavy boot treads catching up faster than I would've liked.

I entered the hallway. It was exactly the same floor plan as the unit upstairs. I was almost out when he caught me around the waist. Before I could retaliate, he hoisted me up, spun me around, and without any preamble dropped me out an open window.

My arms cartwheeled out as I fell. Remaining cognizant of my situation, I kept a firm grip on my gun, which lucky for me was second nature. I hit hard, compressing my legs at the last minute to aid the landing. I rolled a few times, unavoidably crashing into a pile of trash. I was splayed on my back, in a prime position to watch the man jump from the same window, his trench billowing up around him.

He was more prepared for the landing, rolling twice, and was up. He had me by the arm, dragging me off the ground as three men raced around the side of the building, shouting at us, aiming their weapons.

Lasers erupted around us, burning holes in things to our left and right. Moving targets at a distance were harder to hit. "What the fuck?" I yelled, pumping my arms, bobbing, and weaving. The man's hands were off of me, but I followed him, because a) I had no other choice, and b) he hadn't tried to kill me. Yet.

The man turned abruptly, taking off to the right. I spotted what he was running toward half a second later. Both doors to the Q7 lifted on their own as we got closer. "Get in!" he shouted as he leaped inside.

We'd outpaced our chasers, but the laser fire kept coming. I jumped into the passenger side, the door already closing as the mystery man rocketed us up into the air. This craft had ascended far faster than Luce was capable of gaining altitude. He had efficiently gotten us out of handheld-laser range in under three seconds.

Once we were up high enough, I demanded, "Circle around." I gestured out the windshield in front of me. "My ride is down there."

He shook his head, powering us forward with a propulsion blast that shot me backward in my seat.

I still had my Gem out, which I wasted no time leveling at his temple. "Take me to my craft, or I spill your brains and take yours." I was in no mood to dicker.

Daze was out there with those men, and I intended to get him back.

"You shoot me and we both go down. Backtracking is of no service to the kid." He leaned over, hawking a mouthful of blood onto the floor, using his forearm to clean off the rest. He looked like shit.

"I need my ride."

"You can't get it now." Each word came out like a metal scraper grating across a stubborn screwhead. "Tandor has guys swarming the area. They've been waiting for you. And after those laser blasts, the entire Port Station guard will be out in force."

I dropped my arms and pitched my shoulders back, striking my elbows against the seat. "Fuck!" I stamped a boot into his upper dash, mollified as I heard a crack.

The guy shot me a veiled look out of the corner of his eye, but said nothing.

The Q7 was insanely fast, but as predicted, the ride wasn't as smooth. By the time I decided to get another ground view, we were already outside of Port Station, everything below us a blur, the craft vibrating lightly.

My tech phone buzzed in my pocket.

I took off my helmet, tossing it on the ground next to my feet as I fished the phone out, depressing the button. "Ella here. Rennie came down with something. We won't be able to come to dinner after all." My finger dropped the button, and I tried not to choke. I settled for a cough instead.

We didn't have a lot of precode for what happened back there.

Bender's voice came over the line first. "It's Johnny. Sorry to hear that." His tone held an edge. Static issued for a few beats, and then, "I have some medicine I can bring over."

I punched the button. "Not necessary." I could hear the pain in my voice. I knew they could, too. "His dad is taking care of him."

Lockland came on next. "Jerry here. I have the battery extender. I'm happy to bring it by."

He knew I wasn't in my ride, and they both likely knew what had just gone down at Port Station if they were in contact with the guards. Laser fire like that was incredibly rare. I had to think of a response that wouldn't worry them to the point of coming after me.

I darted a glance at the stranger beside me.

He'd taken off his helmet. His dark hair was longer than I'd expected, brushing the collar of his jacket, but other than that, I couldn't see much. I'd lost my chromes somewhere in the mix, and my helmet was on the floor. I tilted my head back. "A neighbor dropped by," I decided on, letting up on the button and giving them static before I hit it again and finished, "We're going to chat for a little bit, and then I'm going to turn in for the night."

"I'll see you for breakfast tomorrow." Bender's voice didn't broker an objection.

"Will do. Ella, out," I half whispered on a long, hollow breath.

Instead of throwing the tech phone as hard as I could against the windshield and watching it explode into a million pieces, which was what I wanted to do, I calmly stuffed it back in my vest pocket. Reclining against the seat, I took in a few measured breaths before I spoke. "How are you planning to get back into the city?"

"I'm not."

I surged up, turning toward him, barely refraining from taking control of the steering levers, scissor-kicking him in the face, and flying this thing myself. "What are you talking about? I have to go home and figure out where Tandor took Daze. I have to make plans. All of those things take place *inside* the city."

I'd utterly failed Daze, and I'd sustained him for only one day.

As a parent, I sucked.

"I know where they took the kid." He spat another wad of blood onto the floor. I ignored it. The asshole deserved everything he'd received for sneaking up on me.

"Then let's go get him." I ran the side of my Gem up and down my thigh in an agitated fashion that reeked of instability. I hadn't felt this out of control in fifteen years. That was the year Bender had me doing runs for him. I was twelve.

"We can't," he grunted. "Unless you have an extra stash of hydro-bombs on you."

"Well, not on me, obviously, but that can be arranged." His eyebrows shot up as he redirected the craft. *East* blinked on the screen. I angled my head out the passenger window, trying to get a bead on the topography. "Where are you going? The ocean is east."

"Yes."

"What the fuck do you mean, *yes?* That's not an answer." The ocean, outside of the protected harbor, especially at the shoreline, was ridiculously dangerous. Fifteen-meter waves were considered small. The sea was a swirling mass of anger and aggression, still pissed off all these years later that it'd been bothered by things hurled at it from outer space. There were many stories about the Flotilla being swallowed up by the insatiable appetite of the water before it got five kilometers outside the bay. There was no way to know for sure.

"You haven't been out of the city much." It wasn't a question.

I crossed my arms, my Gem still gripped in my fist. "I get out of the city all the time, dickhead." At this point, I could forcibly direct the asshole back by gunpoint, and we could enter the city through one of my secret ways. But divulging that kind of info to a stranger was off-limits. I'd do it if he could guarantee we'd get Daze back. "You said you know where they're taking the kid. I can get you into the city, if you agree to take me to him."

"Not tonight."

"Why?"

"They're expecting you."

"How do you know that?"

"The kid was a plant."

I sucked in a breath. Daze had been lying to me?

No. *No no no no no.* "The fuck he was." I'd know it.

"He was. They knew you'd go after the pico."

I shifted abruptly in my seat, my eyebrows drawn, fury rising. I was one second away from hollowing out this guy's neck, or maybe making a nice clean hole through his brain. "I don't get played like that."

"Don't be too hard on the kid." His tone was low and even, but still gritty. "He was a runaway, stole something from Tandor, got caught, and had to do this or die a very painful death. If he didn't get you to the residence within a day, they said they'd kill another kid. Some girl."

"Renata." My voice was devoid of emotion. Daze had lied and said she was already dead. Fisting my hands and beating them bloody on the dash was a solid idea. Instead, I asked, "How the hell do you know all this?"

"I told you, I have someone on the inside."

The man slowed the craft, sliding us right. I leaned forward. In the dim darkness, gigantic waves came in to stark view, crashing against the shoreline. I hadn't seen the edge of the ocean since I was ten or so, when Bender had taken me out here to show me its wrath.

Once had been enough.

As far as I knew, there was nothing out here. Everything within distance of the shoreline had been ravaged, swept out to sea, or pummeled into sand and dust.

The craft rocked unsteadily as he took us over the water, the air currents unstable above the onslaught of tidal waves, shaking us violently. "Your engine is too heavy," I said, trying hard to keep my voice even. "It gives you speed, but in this kind of turbulence, it could upend us and send us spiraling to our deaths." Honestly, in all my imaginings, I'd never thought the ocean would be the thing to kill me. Lasers—or even tasespray—but never the sea. My fist gripped the seat beneath me in an effort to keep myself rooted in the here and now. Watching the ocean roil and surge ten meters below was nothing short of terrifyingly awesome.

The man punched a lever. A soft red effused the space, along with running lights outside. "She has a custom stabilizer."

"She does, does she?" My voice was heavy on the sarcasm. Like a stabilizer was any match for the thunderous sea. He aimed the nose down, dipping fast. I held back the scream rising in my throat, both hands clutching the bottom of the seat as a lifeline, gun and all. "The waves are right beneath us! What the hell are you doing?" The entire windshield was filled with a churning mass of destruction ready to reach up its tendrils of death and yank us under.

At the last moment, he swerved, repositioning us back the way we'd come.

Then I saw it.

The gaping maw of a hollowed-out building. Right on the coast.

I unfurled my fingers from the seat one at a time as the mystery man guided the Q7 expertly into a stall no bigger than the craft itself and shut down the power.

Chapter 16

Once we landed, I sat there like a dummy, panting, my head bowed. But I didn't care. The night had not met any of my expectations, and had been, in its own right, harrowing.

The guy seemed content to wait.

We were parked at least thirty meters from the beach, but the waves crashed like thunder behind us, the echoes of their wrath strumming through my body, pounding like a beating heart through my veins, one after another.

And all I could think was that Daze had played me like a pro.

A fucking *pro*.

"Damn it all to hell." I lifted my head, slapping my hands down on the tops of my legs, my gun driving painfully into my thigh. I barely acknowledged it.

"If you're not more careful, that thing is going to explode on you." He nodded at the Gem.

I curled my lip, not even bothering to answer. Instead, I reached over and lofted the door. I had to *do* something. The space was tight, but it was enough to squeeze by. Heading behind the craft, toward the water, wasn't an option, so I ducked around front.

It was a little trickier for the man to get out, since he was twice my size. I thought I heard a few groans and definitely spotted a limp as he came toward me, which made me feel much better.

"Where to?" I asked. "I'm assuming we're not staying out here."

He moved into the shadows farther away from the water. I followed. A short distance away, a wall loomed, and as we got closer, I spotted a door. It was no ordinary entryway. It was enhanced, made from matte black metal, likely steel mixed with iron, and instead of a knob, it had a spoked wheel set in the middle. The man didn't hesitate to turn it, first cranking it to the right and then to the left. It was too dark to see the exact combination, but there was one.

When the wheel stopped spinning, he yanked the heavy door toward his chest. A popping sound followed, like the building had exhaled. He strained, repositioning himself with both hands curled over the lip, muscling it back enough for us to get through. When he'd achieved his goal, he nodded at me to enter.

As I scooted by, I saw that the door was at least a meter thick.

Once we were both inside, he turned toward a lever jutting from the wall. He pulled it down, and the door slowly shut on its own. Once it was fully closed, with an audible clap, he engaged a deadbolt the size of half my body, sliding it with both hands, adding a little shoulder action, until everything engaged into a massive slot on the side.

The moment the door had closed, the sounds of the ocean disappeared completely.

Nobody was getting in or out of this place.

We were in a bunker of some kind.

It should've worried me, because I didn't know this guy, and this could all be an elaborate plan to murder me, but I was too pissed off and hyped up on adrenaline to be alarmed. I headed down a long hallway ahead of him. "What is this place?" I called as I examined the walls, which looked to be made of concrete. There was just enough light issuing from a few small bulbs near the ceiling for me to see without infrared. I flipped my visor up.

"Head down the stairs," he grunted.

I shuffled down the short flight, which led to another hallway. At the end was a door. Tentatively, I turned the regular knob and pushed it open. It swung without any resistance. "No other external entrances and exits except for the one we just came through, correct?" I asked. Otherwise, the door in front of me would've been locked.

"None that are accessible at the moment."

The room was dark until the man hit a switch on the wall. Light bulbs, covered in protective mesh baskets, blinked on, one by one, sounding like a low drumbeat that started from the right and ended at the far left.

The room was massive.

Crates of supplies were scattered all over, many covered in green and black tarps. Tables and overturned chairs were situated in small groups, some with plates and cups still adorning the surfaces, left behind after the original inhabitants had evacuated quickly. There was a main sitting area, complete with two large couches placed in front of a thigh-high tech table, and an adjoined kitchen space. In the back, sleeping pods were set into the wall, two rows high. The ones on the bottom rolled out, ready for use. A single one on the end with the lid open.

"Military barracks." I glanced at the stranger, stating the obvious. "Most of this building is underground, isn't it? That's why this place survived so close to the ocean."

The man limped toward a massive cooling unit that was shoved against a wall, a utilitarian countertop running next to it, simple metal cabinets above. "Not exactly underground, more like burrowed into the side of a hill." His breath was labored, his words scratchy. Instead of opening the cooling unit, he rummaged through a cabinet next to it. When he found what he was looking for, he turned, a white box with a red lid in hand, and headed toward one of the couches.

If he lifted his pant leg, I was fairly certain I'd see a bruise in the shape of my boot print.

I moved across from him and sat, my Gem out,

barrel up. "Okay, you've got exactly three minutes to tell me who you are, what you want, and why you followed me."

"I wasn't following you." His tone was dismissive as he arranged himself on the couch, ignoring my threating weapon. "I arrived before you. I was already in the closet, remember?" He set the box on the tech table, which was not currently on, and began to shrug off his coat, unable to hide a wince. I glanced inside the open container. It was full of bandages and antiseptic, along with a few auto-inoculations and painkiller darts.

"Two minutes."

After his coat was off, he peeled one of his shirts over his head, leaving a T-shirt behind. Both pieces of clothing were covered in blood. He tossed the long-sleeved shirt aside. His arms were thick and corded with muscle, his biceps jumping as he reached for the box. "I'm an outskirt, here to track down Tandor. I followed you last night because you took the kid. I didn't follow you today. I anticipated your movements and happened to be correct in my assumptions."

My gun stayed steady on my nonmoving target, who acted like he didn't care. But I knew better. Nobody was immune to a laser blast, especially at point-blank range. "You couldn't have followed me yesterday. I would've known. My craft is equipped with radar. I saw you in the area, and I evaded you. I spoofed your system, led you on a chase, and took off."

His head remained down, but his eyes trained upward. They were stark gray, his brown hair drying in slight waves around his face. "The kid had a tracking device behind his left ear."

I lowered my gun, but kept both hands firmly around the barrel as I stood and spun in a circle, my right foot stamping down. "You have to be *fucking* kidding me." My voice was ragged as I took in a long breath, my eyes closing as my head tilted up to the ceiling. It was hard to keep the bravado going when I'd been so plainly had. I felt like throwing up my hands and walking away, but instead, I repositioned them, the muzzle back on its mark, my eyes open and focused. "What's your name? Where did you come from?" I had business to finish.

He ripped open a medi-towel with his teeth, pulled out the damp cloth, and mopped it over his face and nose. The blood melted away instantly, seeping into the cloth like it was supposed to. "Case. South." He tossed the blood-saturated towelette down and reached for another, repeating the process.

"Where south?" There were ports dotted all along the Eastern Seaboard where people had been trying to scrape and survive since the dark days. I'd never bothered with investigating them, since most people migrated up to the city eventually. The city had the most resources, and that was saying a lot, since we basically had shit. I had no idea how people who lived on the outskirts survived for as long as they had.

"What used to be South Carolina."

"Any sunshine down there?"

"Nope."

"Are people better off down there?"

"Nope."

"Why'd you come here?"

He unrolled a large piece of gauze, ripping off two pieces, curling them into tubes, shoving one in each nostril. Once they were securely lodged, he placed his fingers on either side of his bridge and snapped his nose back into place.

The sound was halfway between a hammer on the back of a shell and the slurping sound of a boot being tugged out of the mud. The gauze was instantly drenched dark red.

He leaned his head back, closing his eyes.

Hey. We weren't done here. "If you want me to lower my very precise, never-miss laser, you're going to have to tell me why you're here. Exactly why. With lots of informative words and colorful descriptions."

He didn't bother lifting his head or opening his eyes. "Tandor took over my town less than a year ago. He killed indiscriminately. He succeeded in starting an uprising to bring north. He killed someone close to me. When he left, I followed."

"Is he involved in child slavery?"

"Yes."

I lowered my weapon and sat back down on the couch opposite him. I wasn't going to shoot a hole through someone who wasn't even looking at me, much less putting up a fight. He knew it. I knew it. "What is Tandor hoping to achieve?"

"Total control over the city to further his agenda."

I plucked the roll of gauze off the table and tossed it, hitting him squarely in the chest. It tumbled down, but he caught it before it hit the ground, eyes still closed. "You're going to need another medi-towel and some new gauze. Your nose is a fucking mess." With a disgruntled sigh, he sat up, ripping off two new pieces of gauze. I opened a fresh towel, unraveled it, and handed it to him. It smelled vaguely of Bang and was sticky wet. "You might just want to wad two medi-towels up there and call it a day." I leaned forward to glance in the box. "Is there a numbing agent in here? You might want to use that as well, either darts or mist. It'll probably help you with your knee pain, too." I sat back, barely suppressing a satisfied grin.

He scowled, tugging the first drenched and completely unrecognizable gauze strips out of his nose. They resembled nothing more than two big globs of clotted blood. Then he discarded the gross mess inside a used medi-towel.

In fascination, I watched as the chemicals in the towel consumed the blood from the gauze, leaving it white again in less than twenty seconds. The medi-towel, however, was a deep scarlet, almost overflowing onto the table it was so full. It was hard to believe all that blood could be absorbed by that thin towelette. The wonders of science. To think of where the world should be now, compared to where it actually was, remained heartbreaking.

Once Case had shoved in the new gauze and mopped his face with yet another towel, including his neck, he swept all the bio-waste up into his hand and stood, walking over to a steel trash bin. When he had disposed of everything, he opened the cooling unit. "You want something?"

"I'll take water." He brought over a jug and two carbon molded cups, setting them on the tech table, and sat. I eyed him while he poured the clear liquid. He was taller than Bender, but leaner. He was in expert shape, his leg muscles taut and well-defined, straining his old, faded military fatigues as he sat. He was used to living the hard life and surviving, and it showed. His dark brown hair was longish, cut indiscriminately. His skin had a brown hue. Stubble darkened his chin, indicating he'd been on the road for a few days at least. His jaw was square and stubborn, much like his current expression.

I peeled off my gloves, one at a time, juggling my Gem, and stuffed them into my pockets. Then I picked up the cup and brought it to my lips, relishing the cold water as it hit the back of my throat. Once I was done, I set it down, bracing my elbows on my thighs. The Gem wasn't raised, but I wasn't holstering it anytime soon. "You know, Case, you've only answered a third of my questions. We haven't even scratched the surface. This would go much faster if you would speak more than five words at a time. How'd you find out about this place?" I glanced around. It was clear officials from the city had no idea this existed, or all the supplies would've been long gone. "You're ex-militia, aren't you?" It wasn't really a question. His fatigues, the Q7, and access to this location said it all.

He sat back, assessing me. His eyes gave him away. They compressed at the corners, giving me my answer. He needed a better poker face. "Who said ex?"

Now we were getting someplace, although that was only three words. "You're part of an active militia group in South Carolina? You told me you were an outskirt. Which is it?" The militia was the law-and-order setup in any surviving town.

An outskirt ignored the rules. The militia enforced them.

"Both."

I raised my eyebrows. "Listen, asshole, you dragged me out of that residence, dropped me out a second-story window, and forced me here against my will when I wanted to go home. You know all about Tandor. This entire mess clearly involves me, or he wouldn't have put the kid up to double-crossing me. Keep talking."

I hated that I'd been duped.

God, that hadn't happened in so long.

"I didn't drag you out, I saved you. Tandor's men would've killed you on sight."

I relaxed back into the couch, crossing my legs— my fully operational and mostly pain-free gams. They ached a little from the drop, but at least I wasn't limping. "Why me? Why take the trouble to set up, and potentially kill, a salvager?"

His gray eyes pierced mine. The hairs on my arms started to rise. "That's not who you are."

"What are you talking about?" I uncrossed my legs, sitting up abruptly. There would be no relaxing. "Stop wasting my time. You don't know me, and I don't know you. If you're trying to convince me that we're on the same team, tell me what you have on this creep so I can figure out what needs to be done about it. Instead of leading me around in fucking circles."

"This creep intends to take over the city, and he wants each and every person who could stand in his way eliminated first. He knows about you, and your group, and the power it wields. He wants you gone, and he went for the advantage. He led you to Daze's home, so he could orchestrate things his own way."

I had to make an effort to shut my mouth, since it'd tumbled open a little. "But you got in the way of his plans."

"I got in his way."

"And what does he intend to do once he takes over the city?"

Case shrugged, taking another gulp from his cup, then refilling it from the depleted jug. "My guess, from most of his rantings, is he wants to enslave the population so he can control all of the resources, which he will happily share with only his disciples."

"Enslave them how?"

"Infect them all with Plush."

Chapter 17

"So, let me get this straight." We were a solid twenty minutes into discussing Tandor, and I had begun to pace. I'd made it from the sitting area to a crate of dry-ionized meals toward the back. Just add water and, presto, you had a protein cake—or, more aptly, protein slush. "Tandor has gathered enough bodies and weaponry to take over the city already?" My voice projected just fine in this space. "Then why hasn't he already done so? He's been here at least two months."

"He's patient." Case sat where I'd left him on the couch, his head back, eyes closed. He hadn't moved, nor had he taken a numbing agent. He was in more pain than he was letting on. "He's willing to wait and get it right. Once your group is gone, he moves. He knows how the government operates, and he has people on the inside."

This was big news. I refrained from grabbing my

head in between my palms, and instead made my way back to the couches. "I have to warn my friends. They have no idea this guy is after us or what he's capable of." From what Case had described, this Tandor guy was a freak and a zealot. He'd preached a better life for his followers—at the expense of everyone else.

This wasn't the first or last time the city would encounter such an issue. People in despair were susceptible to influence, and this line of thinking catered to those who cared only about their singular, insular existences. It fed that part of them that frantically wished life could be better than they actually knew was achievable.

"They already know." His voice was strained, more gravelly than it'd been an hour ago. He needed sleep.

"Why do you say that?" I came to a stop behind him.

"Because if they have any smarts at all, they've investigated what just happened in Port Station. Now that Tandor has shown his hand, he has no choice but to move quickly."

I dug in my vest pocket for my tech phone, pulled it out. "It's Ella." I let go of the button and pressed it again. "It's Ella. Anyone there?"

"The signal can't penetrate these walls."

"Then I'll go outside." I moved toward the door.

"Still won't work. We're too far out. No signal amps anywhere near here."

I spun around midstride, my arms flapping. Abject agitation was closing in. "Why in the hell did you bring me here? My family is in danger. I have to go back."

Case lifted his head off the cushion, barely opening his eyes. "If you go now, you'll walk into a trap. He's expecting you to react emotionally."

"I'm not emotional!"

I was, bar none, the most emotional I'd been since the day I'd held my mother's hand as she'd taken her last breath. Goddammit, I didn't do loss well.

"Are your friends smart?" Case asked, leaning forward, cocking his head from side to side as he ran his hand around the back of his neck.

"Of course." I was offended.

"Then they've already taken the necessary precautions. And if they care about you, they're happy you're out of the city at the moment. You can contact them in the morning." He stood and limped toward the sleeping pods.

"That's it?" I called after his retreating back. "We just bunk up here safe and sound while a lunatic child-slavery zealot takes over *my* city?" *And kidnaps my kid.*

Not my kid. Never my kid.

And he wasn't kidnapped, if what Case had told me was true, he was a conspirator.

Fuck.

I followed Case as he shuffled to the pod, the one with the lid already open, and climbed inside. Leaning against the one next to his, I pointedly ignored his wish for peace and quiet as he draped an arm over his eyes. "Last night, did you track the kid and me all the way back to my residence?"

"No. The beacon stopped transmitting in a building by the canals. The signal location was too secure. I couldn't breach it."

Damn straight it was secure.

The tracker must've come off when I made Daze don the helmet. I was momentarily confused. "If Daze was working for Tandor, why were you tracking him? It should've been Tandor's people after me."

"I stole the receiver."

I allowed my eyes to roam over the mystery man whom I still knew next to nothing about. He was militia and a self-proclaimed outskirt. He was from the South, had access to this space, and he wasn't worried about much of anything, judging by his laid-back attitude. Tandor had harmed someone Case loved, so he was here to exact his revenge.

As if sensing my scrutiny, he mumbled, "We'll come up with something in the morning. Go to sleep." He rolled, turning his back to me.

Reluctantly, with nothing else to do, I opened up the pod next to his and got in. The barracks seemed fairly secure, but I had no idea if this guy was telling me the truth about anything. I also didn't know if he would try to harm me during the night, so I curled one hand around my Gem and eased the taser out of its holster with the other. I crossed them on my chest.

I was a light sleeper when I needed to be. If Case decided to try any shit, I'd be ready.

My mind buzzed as I lowered the lid. The things I'd learned in the last hour had been intense. I was in trouble, my team was in trouble, my city was in trouble. And throughout it all, I'd been clueless.

Foolish didn't even come close.

Agreeing to sustainer a street kid within ten minutes of meeting him proved I'd lost my mind. "Next time, I'm going to trust my gut," I grumbled.

What was I talking about?

There wouldn't be a next time.

I blinked. Nothing felt familiar.

But I didn't panic.

This had happened to me before. Many times. Living in this world was always disorienting.

Then it all came flooding back. Port Station, Daze, Tandor, Case, barracks, picos, and quantum drives.

In a rush of pissed-off energy, I rose from the pod, shoving it open with the aid of my foot, my hands still curled around my weapons. Once I was out, I shut the lid and set the weapons on the top with a clatter, massaging my palms, encouraging the feeling to come back. I flipped my wrists back and forth as I turned, stopping midflick. Case was seated at a table, forking something out of a bag. "What? They could've squeezed a trigger just fine."

"Whatever."

I holstered the taser, but kept the Gem out. I wasn't ready to trust yet. It would be a while. If ever. "Let's go."

He stood without argument, carrying his empty container to the trash. After he dumped the contents, he kicked on the button, and the thing gurgled, dicing everything into fine dust in seconds. "I'm assuming you have a way into the city without being seen."

I didn't need to answer the obvious.

Instead, I glanced around. "How did you find out about this place? Everything seems to be in working order, except that tech table, but there are a ton of rations." I walked over to a crate and picked up a bag lying on top. I held up the package. It was a little bigger than my palm and filled with dried flakes. "This has a date before the dark days." I rifled through at least ten more. They all had the same date. "This should all be gone. It's been years." I dropped the one I held back on the pile. "I don't get it."

Case shrugged on his trench. It was similar to Lockland's, except Case's was well worn, shorter, and made of some type of canvas, not synthetic. I assumed it was old military, like everything else. He headed toward the door. He was barely limping. It seemed he was a quick healer. "This place was shown to me a few years back. As far as I know, nobody else knows of its existence."

I followed him out. He was in the hallway before I caught up. "The government sweeps this coast." At least, I thought it did. "They should've seen it."

"It's been covered in sand for over fifty years. Only a small passage free. It's been cleared out by weather in the last ten." We reached the outer door. Case heaved the deadbolt, leaning his shoulder against the wall to get leverage. It finally popped out of its catches, but not without a few grunts of effort. "The government doesn't come out here now. There aren't enough people to spare since the boats left." Case engaged the lever on the wall.

The moment the door creaked open, the crashing of the waves deafened me and the overpowering smell of salt permeated the air. I had to refrain from settling my hands over my ears to block out the sound like a child. It was both terrifying and wondrous. Seeing the ocean up close and personal, it was hard to believe The Water Initiative had ever worked.

Case placed both his palms on the door and pushed, his body straining. He managed to get it open enough for us to slip through. "How many times have you been here?" I had to shout over the din. The sky was brighter than usual, making it easier to see. That happened on some days. I made my way around the side of the Q7, my hand trailing along the craft, the coolness of the carbon under my fingertips feeling safe. The power and sheer magnitude of the sea made me feel small and insignificant. My eyes tracked to the shoreline as the waves arced up in a beautiful dance, the water murky and dark, turbulent and wild, crashing down in an instant. The sound was like a hydro-bomb exploding at short range, only to be sucked back into the abyss, never ceasing, the dance beginning all over again.

It was amazing to me that Earth could take so much abuse and not crack, the ground opening beneath the constant battering, swallowing us once and for all.

Behind me, Case entered the craft.

With reluctance, I forced my gaze away from the sea. Case had parked in a remnant of what used to be another room of the bunker. Heaps of sand were piled in various corners, backing up Case's story about it being covered up for all those years. The entire front end of the building had been destroyed. A tidal wave of tsunami proportions was my guess. Maybe more than one.

In order to see us, another craft would have had to be positioned out front, above the ocean. Since most crafts wouldn't venture out there, for fear of wind shear and updraft, it was a great hiding spot.

Perfect, really.

I lifted the door and slid into the seat, jamming my arms through the shoulder harness, clipping it in front of me. After the ride last night, I was anticipating some twists and turns. And who was I if I didn't follow my own advice? Thinking of Daze pissed me off all over again.

Case started the props and backed us out, spinning and lofting us into the air efficiently. The wind caused slight turbulence, but overall it wasn't a problem.

It was clear Case was an excellent pilot.

Most people couldn't fly a dronecraft smoothly. Keeping things steady was an art form. It took concentration and input from both halves of your brain, your hands working the levers in tandem. If you overcompensated on either pitch or roll, you died in a fiery crash. Back before the dark days, crafts were flown exclusively on autopilot, monitored constantly by satellites. Dronecraft had elaborate computer systems, which were continuously being updated via the sky. People had, in every aspect of their lives, given themselves over to sophisticated systems and tech. Accidents by any flying craft almost never happened. It must've been a happy world with nothing much to worry about.

"Where to?" Case asked. The main entrance to the city was open, but it would be monitored.

"You're dropping me off outside, and I'm making my way in on my own," I countered.

"Bullshit."

I gave him a look. A cross between irritation and contempt. "I'm not compromising anything to you. Getting you in by a secret route would do just that."

"I saved your life last night."

"The hell you did. You tossed me out a window. I could've taken on whoever was coming up the stairs *and* gotten to my craft. You fucked me over, *and* I could've broken my neck. I owe you nothing."

"Fine. You fly and blindfold me. You reveal nothing."

"I can't recover Luce until blackout." I wondered if my craft was even still there. They could've blown her up by now. Or Tandor's henchmen could've stripped her down. They wouldn't have gotten very far, but still. She could be irreparably damaged.

He sighed. "I'm talking about you flying this." Case buzzed us over a thick forest of twisted trees, branches bare, aching to feel the sunshine on their blackened skin once again. I didn't recognize the area, but I knew we were east.

We had a hidden entrance on the east side of the city. I rested my leg on the middle console. There was never enough room in these things. "You want me to fly your Q7? You can't be serious."

"Deadly."

"That means you're assuming I can pilot this thing, no questions asked." I could. That wasn't even up for debate. But this guy didn't know that. Each dronecraft had its own nuances. If he'd seen Daze and me at the gorge, and by his own admission, he had been tracking me, he knew I flew an A1.

"Can't you?"

"Of course I can." Why did this guy always make me sound so indignant? Not only sound it, but feel it. Like I had something to prove. It was getting on my nerves.

"If I'm blindfolded and you're flying, no secrets are revealed." His voice was tired. My guess was he'd been up for a few days straight before his sleep last night.

"Once we're in, we go our separate ways."

"Fine."

"How do I know you won't peek?" I asked. It was a logical question.

He met me with a stare that carried weight. It covered my body like the blanket I'd tossed on Daze and was just as nauseating. "I give you my word."

Taking him at his word could get me killed, but I had little choice at this point. I nodded. "Set her down."

Chapter 18

The lonely patch of ground we landed on was desolate to say the least. We both opened our doors at the same time, light drizzle pattering from the sky. The air carried a hint of salt, but no echoes of the waves. We'd traveled inland a few kilometers. "We're farther south than I thought," I said as I walked around the front of the craft. "I lost track after Port Station."

"We're approximately fourteen kilometers southeast of the city."

We passed each other. I had to look up to see his face, which irritated me. But honestly, what wasn't irritating about this situation? His expression was bland. I hated not being able to read him. He was tricky and likely withholding a lot of necessary information. But I didn't feel threatened. If I had, I would've incapacitated him already.

I wasn't sure what I felt. Uneasy? Angry?

If I was being honest, most of my anger was

directed at Daze and this guy Tandor for wanting to take over my city and forcing the kid to play me. But I also held a nugget of pissed off for this out-of-towner militia man who knew more than I did about what was going on in my own town.

I situated myself into the pilot's seat and pulled the door down with more force than necessary, causing it to crack loudly. The controls looked similar to Luce's, but there were some differences. The levers had buttons on the top. I had no idea what they were for, but I wasn't about to ask. This was going to be a learn as-I-go endeavor. I punched the craft on and toggled a switch that retracted the landing gear, lofting us a meter off the ground.

The response time was quicker than my craft. I made note of that so I didn't overshoot. I glanced pointedly at Case, waiting for him to cover himself up with something.

He frowned. "What? You want me blindfolded now? We're fourteen kilometers away. You hardly have a secret route from this patch of forest to the city."

I drummed my fingertips, now gloved, on my thigh. "Either you find something to cover your eyes, or we stay right where we are."

His jaw ticked. "Do you even know how to get to the city from here?"

"Unless the fractured buildings are obscured by a magical force field, I think I can figure it out. Go north thirteen kilometers and take a left. What have you got in here to use as a blindfold?" I turned to rummage around in the backseat. It was shamefully clear of clutter. My head jerked toward Case. "Where's all your stuff?" He shrugged. He hadn't bothered to clip into the harness and wasn't going to look in the backseat where I was currently jabbing an angry finger. "People can actually sit back here."

His lips quirked. It was the most emotion I'd seen thus far. "Yank the back of the seat down."

I had to lift my hips, stretch, and twist to finally grasp the top of the seat, slamming it down.

Supplies, weapons, and other utilitarian things spilled out. With relief, I said, "Whew, for a second there I thought you were an amateur."

"Nope." His voice was calm and cool. "I just prefer people be able to ride when necessary."

I ignored him, searching for something that would cover his face fully. I found it in the form of some sort of shiny insulated cover-up. When I grasped it, the material crinkled in my hand, making an irritating noise. "Is this a Teflon suit? Or what's left of one?" I held it up. It looked like it'd had pants attached at some point, but they'd been sheared off, the ends ragged, threads dangling. He wouldn't be able to see through it *and* it would make him sweat. Perfect. I thrust it at him. "Tie that around your face."

He gave me a long look but complied, the material making satisfying rasping noises as he tied the arms in a big knot at the back of his head. Once he was done, he held up his hands. "Are we good?"

I waved an open palm in front of his face. He didn't react. "We're good." I settled into the driver's seat, getting comfortable, wrapping my hands around each of the controls. They were bigger and more cumbersome than Luce's, but I'd deal. I punched the props up a notch as I eased back with my left hand, at the same time maneuvering my right hand forward.

We sailed smoothly into the air, the craft easing north as I accelerated.

Man, this felt good. "What do you call her?" I asked as I took us higher, not another craft in sight as far as I could see.

"I don't." His voice was pleasingly muffled.

My eyebrows shot up. "You didn't name your craft?"

"Nope."

As I gained altitude, the ride smoothed out. I eased off the throttle. "Seven." The info panel digitized all of the components, a few more than Luce had, such as barometric pressure and a terrain monitor. "That's what I'm going to call her." We were traveling at a hundred and twenty kilometers an hour, which was a fairly standard cruising speed at forty meters above ground. I knew the Q7's were built for speed. I waved my right hand in front of Case's face again, just for fun. He didn't react. "How fast can she go?"

"With or without hydrogen injection?"

My face showed my surprise, but Case couldn't see it. I was careful not to allow my voice to mirror my reaction. Luce had a hydrogen boost as well, but it wasn't anything that came standard with dronecraft, even the later models. Vaporized fuel was hazardous, especially during a crash. Having it on board meant that the chances the craft would blow up upon impact were almost a hundred percent. Not good for the insurance companies.

That meant Case was either a talented mechanic, or he knew someone who was.

I settled on, "Without boost."

"Over two hundred, but it gets touchy to steer."

I accelerated past one-fifty to one-eighty.

The topography beneath us rapidly began to change. Single-family homes decimated in the aftermath of the meteor began to spring up. They were nothing more than shells. Hunks of roofs and other housing materials lay scattered across the expanses, turned up at odd angles, like scattered bones. Remnants of walls, less than a meter high, gave ghostly reminders of what had once been.

It was always hard to see and made me think, once again, of all the loss the world had endured over the last half century.

So much loss.

We flew in silence for a while. Then I decided it might be best to pump Case for as much information as I could before we parted ways. "You said you know where they took Daze last night. Is that where Tandor has his operations set up?"

"No, the bastard keeps changing his location." The material crinkled as he readjusted. It was too bad Case couldn't see my happy face.

"Do you have a solid plan for defeating him?"

"I'm assuming a laser blast to the temple will do the trick."

"When he's gone, will his followers rise up and see this thing through?"

"One or two might pose a problem, but I'm fairly certain I can be convincing to the contrary with enough force." His voice held an edge I couldn't name. It wasn't as much angry as it was resolute. Or a combination of the two. Tandor had made him mad. There was no doubt that Case had the conviction and the means to back up his claims of bodily harm.

"Why warn me last night, instead of just retaliating?" I asked. "If you knew the pico was a plant, why not wait outside for them to grab me, and then follow them back to Tandor?"

"I didn't think you'd bring the boy with you."

I pursed my lips, angling the craft slightly northwest. "So you modified your plan when you saw us together?" That seemed a little implausible. "To survive in our world, you have to be tough. I wasn't going to baby the kid."

"You didn't take him inside." Case brought his hands under the material, making tons of noise, likely to mop the saturation.

"No, I didn't," I agreed. "I decided it was best for him to stay outside. I was supposed to be in and out in under ten. The kid would've held me up." Some plan that turned out to be. "I'm still not following. What was your actual goal?"

"My plan was to get you both out unharmed, but you separated before I could reach you." He shrugged. "I decided to go in, because the kid will remain alive to use as a bargaining chip as long as you're still around. If I'd taken him and left you there, you would've been killed, and Tandor would've achieved his intended objective."

My head twisted in Case's direction as I snorted. It was a loud, aggressive sound. "I wouldn't have died. You know nothing about me. And what do you mean keep him alive? Daze is working for Tandor. The kid lied to me because Tandor asked him to. Of course they'd keep him alive."

Case shook his head, the material slipping. He resecured it in back and slid his hands under to tent it up so he could talk more freely. I narrowed my eyes, inspecting to make sure he wasn't peeking. "I told you already, the kid was caught stealing. If he hadn't played his part, they would've killed him and his friend. Painfully. It wasn't his choice."

"It was his choice," I countered. "He could've confided in me once he was in my craft. He had ample opportunity later on. I would've helped him."

"He didn't know you." Case's tone was resolute and unbending, his reaction immediately making me think he'd been a street kid himself. "Why would he feel he could trust you after only a few hours?"

The craggy outline of the broken skyline became visible in front of me, silhouetted in the distance, dark clouds swirling, providing a sinister backdrop as rain pelted the windshield. It was hard to imagine how this metropolis once looked in its prime, with megascrapers dotting the horizon, the easy rise and fall of the buildings in between, bustling dronecraft in their appropriate lanes, hypertubes and air buses moving large groups of people to where they needed to go. The streets vibrant and busy.

It was as if the planet had forgotten as well.

My brain circled back to the kid. I wasn't the forgiving type. "I gave Daze every reason to trust me. He could've ratted Tandor out any time before we arrived at Port Station." The kid had been reluctant in the end, but he'd followed through with the plan. Breaking my trust was right up there with putting a gun to my head and threatening to pull the trigger.

Case brought his leg up to the console. I wasn't the only one who needed stretching room. "The kid was a pawn to get to you."

"That may be true, but that doesn't mean I have to like it. Daze had a choice. He chose Tandor."

"He chose saving his own neck and his friend's life. You would've done the same at his age, as I would've."

"You were a street kid." It wasn't a question.

"I was."

"Yeah, so was I." The difference was I never would've sold Bender out. Not even if I'd known him less than a day, and I'd been Daze's Bender. Daze had chosen wrong.

Case didn't comment. "Are we getting close?" He was irritated. "This thing is going to asphyxiate me."

I stifled a snicker. "We're closing in. I'm bringing her down outside the east wall."

"I don't care where you go, just do it soon."

"I can't believe you never named your craft."

"Didn't occur to me."

As the city loomed closer, I reached into my vest and pulled out my tech phone. "It's Ella—"

Case interrupted me. "Don't use your regular channels," he warned. "They're monitoring them."

I took him at his word and dialed the phone to channel four and depressed the button. "Larry, it's Kate." I popped my finger off and waited. After twenty seconds, I tried again. "It's Kate. Anybody out there?" No answer. I thumbed the dial to channel seven and brought it back up to my mouth. "Don, it's Maggie. I need to get a hold of you about breakfast." Nothing. I swore, pocketing the phone. "How do they know so much about us in such a short period of time?"

"One of your friends got involved in something over his head. They were able to get information out of him."

My head snapped in his direction. "What are you talking about? Who?"

"A guy named Darby."

I reacted so swiftly the dronecraft bounced in the air before I could regain control. My breath came in shallow, measured increments. "How and when did they get information from him?" My voice was a step away from cracking.

"As far as I know, a few weeks ago. They've got this laboratory or something set up in the canals. He thinks he's participating in something about Plush, but it's just a ruse."

I took my hands off the levers and slammed my fists into either side of the dashboard. The drone jumped and rocked, but I didn't care. "Fuck!" This went so much deeper than I'd anticipated.

"Try not to crash," he said wryly. "I plan on living for at least a few more years."

I leveled us out, reclining my head back against the seat. My helmet was still on the passenger side, at Case's feet, where I'd left it the night before. "How exactly did they get him to talk?"

I closed my eyes.

I didn't want to hear it.

"Babble."

I couldn't reveal to this stranger that I'd just taken Darby into my home and shared my deepest secrets with him—assuming that if the government didn't have Babble, no one would.

Static came over the line. I reached for my phone just as Bender's words filled the craft. "Maggie, it's Sam." His voice conveyed his mood even through the tiny mic. Happiness wasn't a normal emotion for him, but raw impatience wasn't either. "Your breakfast is getting cold."

"On my way," I replied with the button down. "Overslept."

"Come in the back door. Front's locked."

I couldn't risk asking much over the radio waves, but I tried. "Is the entire family going to be there?"

"No. Just Don." Static. "See you in a few."

"Will do. Maggie, out." I stuffed the phone back in my vest.

"Trouble?"

I was in no mood to discuss anything about myself with this stranger. "We're landing soon. Brace yourself."

"Why do I need to—"

I whipped Seven around in a wide arc, jamming my hand to the right while aiming my left hard toward the floor, dropping altitude while turning. Then I began to back her up quickly. I didn't take as much pleasure in seeing Case's hands splayed on the console in front of him and hearing him gasp, the ridiculous fabric covering his eyes crunching and crinkling, because I was furious. My family was in harm's way and I'd had no idea. "Nobody said getting to this entrance was going to be easy."

Chapter 19

Entering on the east side took finesse. I guided Seven in between obstacles in reverse, bringing her down on the dead earth right outside of a shattered building.

This was the only entryway we had that wasn't radio controlled, operated by a switch on the wall itself. Once Seven was stabilized, I scooped up my helmet, settling it on my head as I popped open the door. "Stay here, and don't even think about peeking. We're almost in."

Case grunted in response.

At the building, I ran my hands over the expanse, searching for the toggle that would open things up. It was well hidden for a reason, and I could never remember exactly which quadrant it was located in. We hardly ever used this entrance, since none of us came from the east very often. This particular section of the wall was a graphene composite mix, with lots of bumps and burrows, making it ideal to modify. I finally found what I was looking for and flipped the tiny switch that was set up under a deep groove. Then I took a few steps back.

The wall began to swing upward and outward.

I headed back to the craft. The ground was rocky and waterlogged, but stable under my boots. It would take some time for the passageway to reach its full height. I slid in, closed the door, and engaged the props. Seven hovered a meter off the ground.

Once the opening was at max height, I crept her in backward.

The space was tight.

There was barely enough room on each side to squeeze her through. Darkness crept over her like an advancing cloud as I eased into the space, leaving the outside behind. Engaging the landing gear, I set her down four meters in. Satisfied with her placement, I punched her off.

We'd landed in the lower floor of another building, but this one wasn't a parking garage. It used to be an auditorium of some kind. The vaulted ceiling soared high above our heads, seats fanning up a short incline. Several balconies lined the back wall. Now, other than a few scattered chairs here and there, the space was empty.

My footsteps echoed as I made my way across the stage to close the passageway.

I hit the button, and the door began to shut. Then I made my way toward a panel on the wall. This one was disguised behind an old video monitor. I flipped the screen and punched in a sequence of numbers. The light above the small board flashed yellow, then began to blink.

I was over the blink.

"Can I undo my blindfold now?" Case called from the craft.

"Nope," I said as I made my way back, scanning the auditorium in front of us, waiting for Lockland to activate the next passageway. I couldn't do it from this craft. I'd had to back Seven in, because the angle we needed to make the exit was too tight to maneuver in a full circle. I got in the pilot side. "I'm late for breakfast, so you're going to keep that on until I say so." My plan was to take the craft all the way to Bender's, land on the roof next door and make Case fly away before he saw where I was headed.

It was the fastest way to achieve my goals, if not exactly the smartest.

Case remained quiet.

He looked completely comical sitting there with his face wrapped in Teflon. While we waited, I pondered what he'd told me about Darby.

If Tandor had given Darby Babble a few weeks ago, Darby had likely compromised only himself and a few of our routes. But there was no way to be certain. There was a strong possibility he hadn't even realized he'd been injected, and he wouldn't remember anything he'd said.

It was a clusterfuck, and the implications were vast.

I ran a hand over my face, settling it around my mouth for a moment. I felt like screaming. How did we miss something this big? Darby was so excited about his research and the possibility of helping people, and it was all a big, fat lie.

The light on the back of the auditorium finally went green. Immediately after, the wall began to retract.

Case asked, "What's that sound?"

"Our way out."

"I thought we just entered." His voice bordered on done. I was actually surprised Case had gone along with everything thus far. This was a man not used to taking orders from anyone, and here I was flying his craft and calling the shots. If he could actually see what I was about to do, he'd insist on taking the controls.

"We did. Now we have to go through one more secured door to get back outside." I eased Seven off the stage, angling her ninety degrees straight up and to the left, quickly and precisely, then lowered her to a forty-five-degree angle as I followed the short rise up and out. The sound of her fans echoing around the empty space was exceptionally loud, not to mention we'd been tossed back in our seats.

"What the hell is going on?" Case yelled, reaching up to rip off his blindfold.

My arm shot out to stay his movements, gripping his tensed forearm. "Don't remove that unless you're looking for a tase to the chest." My hand snatched back to the controls so the craft didn't falter. "Hang tight. We're almost out."

Case complied, but there was a distinct snarl coming from underneath the fabric. I could barely hear it above the prop noise, which was a bonus. I passed through the narrow exit, almost scraping both sides, and immediately turned right onto the street, gaining altitude as I went.

I headed west.

After a few kilometers, I reached over and snatched the blindfold off Case's face. It came away easily. Half-standing buildings whizzed by as rain dashed against the windshield. The only other craft in sight was high above us, heading north.

I glanced over at Case, moisture actively dripping down the sides of his face. "We'll be at our destination in a few minutes. Once I land, you assume the controls. Get up and out immediately." He gave me a look. The one where his head barely moved, but his gray eyes said it all, narrowing at the edges, effectively calling me out as clueless. I was getting fantastically tired of that expression. "Listen, I know you think you're above us because you managed to track me down. But you underestimate me and my crew and what we can do. We will have no problem finding Tandor and his people and eradicating them from this city without your help."

He stared straight ahead. "I don't think I'm above you. But you're out of your league with this one. He's more dangerous than you think."

"Thanks for the fair warning." I turned the craft north, lofting us higher. I was going to miss the fluid efficiency of these controls, but I ached to get Luce back. She'd been with me since the beginning. We were a team.

"We could help each other." His words sounded sincere, even though they'd been uttered in a raspy tone.

I shook my head. "We don't work with outsiders. Lessons learned from years of broken trusts."

He glanced at me, this time his expression clear with no eye-narrowing. "I have information you need."

"I don't make it a habit of owing anyone anything. Like I said, we have feelers out all over the city. My crew will have the necessary information once I get back. We part ways on a rooftop. If you get to Tandor first, great. If we do, fine. Either way, the threat will be eradicated and we all go back to normal."

Once I was within three blocks of my destination, I eased off the street, gliding over the remains of several buildings. The Middle was located between two swaths where buildings had been razed. The people here knew me and begrudgingly allowed me entrance into Bender's sanctioned area, but not much else.

As I lowered Seven onto the building, Case warned, his voice abrasive, "You're making a mistake."

I punched the landing gear and set her down cleanly. "Then that's my mistake to make." I popped the door, leaving her idling. "You have about two minutes to get this craft off this roof before the occupant of this building is up here with a laser that puts my Gem to shame." I climbed out, turning at the last minute to reach down under the dash, ignoring Case's massive thighs, which were now in my face as he made his way over the console, and peeled off my jammer, flipping it in my hand. It was no bigger than the size of a fingernail. Backing away, I rolled it between my index finger and thumb, showing it to him. "Hope you don't mind, but I jammed your radio and video feed, along with your recorder." I winked, saluting him with three fingers, grinning at his furious expression. "Have a good day."

Behind me, the door to the roof banged opened, as expected.

I was already moving, jogging toward the edge of the building as Case took my words to heart and hoisted Seven into the air, a rush of wind billowing at my heels.

A moment later, I leaped onto Bender's roof, straining with all my might to close the gap. I somersaulted as I landed and was up and running toward safety a moment later. Luckily, the laser fire coming from the next roof wasn't aimed at me. Instead, it was pointed at the craft speeding away, an angry voice calling, "Don't come back here! You're not welcome!"

I chortled as I slid to a stop in front of the barricade. "How do you like me now, Case?" I directed my light laser into the appropriate pin hole. I was in front of the door before it fully engaged, then inside, slamming it closed as shouts from the angry neighbor continued to erupt from the other roof, even though Case was long gone.

Bender was waiting for me at the bottom. That was unusual, but what wasn't these days? His face was grim.

I hurried down the last flight, taking the steps three at a time. "What is it?"

"They have Darby." He dropped his arms and stalked inside.

I hurried after. "Tandor? We'll track him down and get Darby back—"

"The government."

I lost my footing for a moment and stumbled before righting myself. Yanking off my helmet, I tossed it carelessly onto a table as we entered Bender's workroom. "The government? Why would they want Darby?"

He walked to his stool and sat, crossing his arms, his muscles bulging. "You tell me."

"What the hell is that supposed to mean?" I stopped in front of him, legs splayed. I was up for a fight, if that's what he wanted.

"He was involved in something illegal."

"I wouldn't exactly classify it as illegal," I countered. "And I only found out a day and a half ago. He believed he was helping, doing something good, and Tandor and his assholes double-crossed him. But none of that had anything to do with the government, as far as I know."

"Why didn't you say anything?" His voice held accusation, but I knew he was stressed. So was I.

I ran a hand through my hair, my gloves catching on the wet strands. I peeled them off and tossed them down. This was going to be a long discussion. "We don't share everything with each other for good reasons. The less people know, the better. You were the first one to teach me that." I gazed at him pointedly. "Darby confided in me that the reason he was in the canals the other night was because he'd met someone who believed they were on to a cure for Plush. Darby seemed to think whatever they were doing was working and that maybe the effects of the drug could be reversed—seekers possibly healed. I just found out on the ride back here that Tandor set it all up, duping Darby. And of course, that was the first thing I was going to share with you when I arrived." Bender's dark eyes scrutinized, flicking over me like he wasn't sure what to believe. I kicked the chair in front of me, making it skitter along the floor, bouncing off a pillar before it came to a clattering stop. "What? You think I'm lying? You think I'd turn on you? What the hell? I got hijacked in Port Station, found out the kid was a mole, and almost died being tossed out a two-story window. After all that, here I am, back here as soon as I possibly could be."

Lockland strode in through an open doorway across the room, holding a cup of steaming liquid, likely amino tea. "Nobody thinks you're lying. Calm down. We heard what happened last night, and all this shit is too sudden. Everyone's on edge. We should've had more warning that something this big was going on."

He slid a chair over and sat. "Tell us what happened. From the beginning. We'll figure it out."

"Fine." I glared in Bender's direction. "But once I'm done, we waste no time going after Tandor. It's more than just a slavery ring. This guy wants control of the city. He's here for a takeover."

"We know that already," Bender replied, this time with a modicum of compassion rather than disdain. "A guard in Port Station took down one of his guys last night. Got him to talk before he took him out. It looks like Tandor is definitely planning a coup."

Lockland shook his head. "How the fuck didn't we know about this? It was right under our noses. I run the security in this operation. This is on me."

"No, it's on all of us," I countered, leaning back, crossing my arms. "We didn't know, because this guy figured out how we operate and considers us a major threat. He took his time, came into town quietly, stayed under the radar, and targeted us directly. Starting with Darby, and then the kid." I refrained from yanking out my hair, but just barely. "They somehow knew I would take the kid. I don't know how they knew, since I didn't even realize it until the last minute." I met Bender's steely gaze, then Lockland's inquiring one. "The kid was wearing a tracker. The only thing that kept them from following us directly to my place was I made Daze wear a helmet. It must have knocked the thing off." I braced my hands against the cold graphene wall, bowing my head. "That and Case."

"Who the hell is Case?" Bender growled.

I dropped my hands and turned. "He's an outskirt, likely militia. He's the one who hijacked me and tossed me out the window. The asshole knows a lot we don't, but he told me enough."

Chapter 20

"He let you fly his Q7?" Lockland's voice held skepticism. I'd just finished laying out the story, along with everything Case had told me during our brief time together.

"Not only *let* me," I said. "He offered. I agreed, but only if he wore a blindfold."

"Teflon was a nice choice," Bender snorted. "Did he know you had a jammer?"

"Hell no. I was stealthy about it." I dug the thing out of my pocket, grinning. "I had the pleasure of showing him as I pried it out from under his dash." I held it up like the prize it was.

Lockland stopped pacing, which he'd taken up as I'd let the story unfold. "These guys know too much about us." He glanced from me to Bender. "This means we have to go deep undercover until we eliminate the threat, effective once we're done here."

I sat, slumping forward in my chair. "This is all my

fault, and because of it, everything I've worked so hard for all these years is going to go up like a fucking hydro-bomb." I glanced up at Lockland. "I took Daze in and led him and Darby back to my private residence. I have things there that would sentence me to an acid bath every day for a month. Shit you guys don't even know about it." I held up my hand. "And don't ask, because I'm not sharing. Not to mention poor Darby. He is the nicest among us, striving to be a decent human every single day of his life. Who knows what they're going to do with him now? He could be dead already."

"He's not dead. The government will hold him for a while, but they won't kill him. They have nothing on him." Lockland stopped in front of a shelving unit full of containers of vaporized fuel, looking pensive. We were all on edge.

Bender drummed his fists on the table before swiping his arm across it, sending the contents flying. "This guy is going down."

"That, he is," I agreed, standing. "Then, once he's out of the way, we get Darby back. Whatever it takes."

"Holly, it might be better if you stayed out of sight while we handle this Tandor ourselves," Lockland declared.

"*What?* You can't be serious." I readied for a fight. "I brought this insanity to our doorstep by taking the kid. I was the one who let my guard down. It won't happen again, but you're not pushing me out. I'm in this to the end."

"It has nothing to do with pushing you out." Lockland sighed. "You're a liability now. You're number one on this guy's radar. And if they you find you, they'll kill you, no negotiation, no trades. It's like the outskirt said—if you go after Tandor, you're playing right into his agenda. He probably won't rise up until you're gone, and we need to stave that off for as long as possible."

"Bullshit," I huffed. "And don't quote this outskirt back to me. If Tandor knows about me, he knows about the two of you." I waggled two fingers between them, my eyes following. "He's targeting us as a group, not just me." We were well known in the city.

"I agree," Bender said. "He went after her first because he knew she would take the kid. Neither of us would've done that. It was an easy way to infiltrate without making waves. If it hadn't worked, he would've tried something else."

I rolled my eyes upward, praying for patience. "You took me in, remember?" My head did a full bob in Bender's direction. It was hard to believe I had to remind him. "You're not immune to a street kid's plight. All you had to do was look into my misty green nine-year-old eyes, and you buckled like an aluminum trash bin. I admit it, I had a moment of weakness. I can promise you, it won't happen again. My gut isn't usually wrong, but in this case, it was. I put us in jeopardy. I apologize. But I'm not heading out of the game, and I refuse to run. I don't mind going under deep cover. We can achieve a lot from there. But I'm not leaving this city. I stay and fight right along next to you."

"Fine, you stay. But we're all going deep under cover," Lockland said. "And when I say deep under, I mean literally. We're going underground."

"Damn," I muttered. "I hate it down there."

"Too bad. That's where we need to be," Lockland replied. "I've already started hauling my equipment down. I'll be set up in three hours. Holly, you take the space farthest south. Bender, you take The North. I'll stay central." He reached into his pocket and withdrew two small tech phones. They were jet-black and had only one dial. "These are modified with a voice scramble. We go by Grace, Sean"—he nodded at Bender—"and Alex. Use them sparingly. They are super-low-frequency magnetic, so underground won't be an issue, and they're channel specific. I've got feelers out, so we should have intel about Tandor's whereabouts soon. We begin operations after blackout."

"Before I go under," Bender said, "I'll hit the skells and ask around." Before Lockland or I could object, he held up a fist. "Nobody's gonna take me down in plain sight. I'll slip underground after that."

"What about weapons?" I asked. "Case mentioned something about needing a cache of hydro-bombs to take them out. My guess is whoever this Tandor is, he's heavily armored with lots of back up."

"You couldn't get more out of this guy?" Bender asked, settling back on his stool with a jug of brown liquid in his lap.

"I could've, if I'd wanted to owe him. I didn't."

"Tell me more about this place by the sea," Lockland said. "Is it somewhere we can penetrate?"

I shook my head. "The door in had a rolling code, and I'm pretty sure if we got it wrong, it would blow. There were likely other security measures inside, but I was hopped up on adrenaline and not thinking straight, so I didn't look. It's too risky."

Lockland nodded. He'd expected an equivalent answer. "If this guy is militia, it has to be protected."

"Hell, if this guy's an outskirt, it's triple bugged," Bender said, taking a swig of aminos. Bender burned a lot of calories in a day.

I made my way to the cooling unit. I should've swiped some of the dry-ionized food from the bunker. The mush was decidedly better than any protein cake. Without another option, I took two blocks out and settled against the counter as I ate. I was having a hard time redirecting my brain away from the fact that I could lose my residence to the government if Darby talked—if I hadn't already. With everything confiscated, I'd be back at square one around here, living like a pauper—that is, if I wasn't arrested and doused with acid for all my illegal activities.

"What about the kid?" Bender asked.

I looked up, startled at his tone. He sounded worried. "What about him? He betrayed us, and he's back where he belongs."

"From what you told us, he had no choice. They were going to kill him and his friend."

I clapped the crumbs off my fingers, my throat thick. "He had a choice when he got into my craft. Then he had a choice when he woke up fed, clean, and rested. Then he had a choice when he stood in this very room and drew us a map so we could create a plan—one that was going to lead to my damn death." My tone was fierce. "Scratch that, to all our deaths, including everyone in the city, except for the asshole zealot and his crew. Those were his choices, and he failed every single one of them."

Bender held my gaze for less than three seconds before he dropped it, nodding. He upended the jug, finishing it off, down to the last nasty brown drop. Once he was done, he dragged a forearm over his mouth. "We roll in five."

Leaving Luce behind was harder than I'd thought it'd be. Lockland had assured me that the guards he'd bribed in Port Station would keep her intact until this was over. But I had my doubts.

Lockland dropped me off in a remote location near the canals. We had several safe places underground, inside the zoom tunnels. The tunnels were where our ancestors accessed the mag-lev trains, riding on efficient people conveyors, quickly passing from hypertube to hypertube. There were millions of riders per day in every major city, so the network had been vast. This city had been one of the meccas, shuttling folks across the country in a matter of hours. Mag-lev technology had revolutionized travel. The evacuated tubes removed all wind resistance, and the trains operated on magnetic levitation, which meant they basically rode on air. They'd been super fast, safe, and affordable.

In order to board a train, you had to enter through an airlock, where you transitioned from normal atmosphere to pressurized. In the aftermath of the meteor, most of the underground stations had filled with water or collapsed, but there were a handful of hypertubes that remained free and clear because they had been sealed during the event and had somehow managed to escape the path of destruction.

It'd taken us years to find these sites and longer to make them operational and secure. We rarely used them, as they were in poor condition for the most part, and it took a hell of a lot of work to reach to them. They were meant to be occupied only during times of heightened emergency. Like these.

Darby knew they existed, of course, but he'd never been to the three we were heading to now, as far as we knew. He had his underground location set up near The Middle, which had been fabricated to power his tech gear.

"Dammit, Darby," I muttered as I moved through the streets toward the building that would lead me underground, picking my way over debris and dodging deep ruts filled with rusty red water. "Why did you have to be so trusting? Always wanting to help people." Caring got you in trouble every time.

A noise came from my right.

I backed myself against the building I was in the process of passing, my eyes scanning the area through my visor, searching for a heat signature. I couldn't detect one, but that didn't mean it was clear. The rain was heavy and cold, and it would alter a heat signature if the person was chilled.

After a long minute, a seeker stumbled into view.

The signature was almost solid blue, only a tiny bit of orange at the center. Seekers didn't care about how they dressed or if they kept warm, they just mindlessly searched for their next fix. I waited for the female to maneuver off in the other direction.

I was close to my destination, and I wasn't taking any chances.

Once underground, I would wait for a radio signal from Lockland. His main job was security, but he was also the point of contact for our group and the government. He didn't share his insiders with us for good reason, but I knew he paid them well. The payments oftentimes came from my salvages.

That's how we worked. It kept us all alive.

I ran my hand along the building as I picked up the pace, my gloves leaving a trail of wet lines. When I got to the end, I was forced to leap across a large crack full of murky water. This was the very edge of the canals. A place where I felt right at home. I tried not to dwell on the possible loss of my residence, which was less than a kilometer away. Thinking about it got me sweaty and angry all over again.

At the next street, I turned left, hustling toward my destination.

Since the rain was falling hard and the clouds were thick, the dimmer light provided good cover. I arrived at the side entrance of a nondescript building, less than half of it still standing, and ducked inside. The stairwell to my right had been covered by a large piece of scrap metal, placed at an angle to look like it'd been there since the disaster.

I knew better as I shimmied through the small opening made by the haphazard placement. Once inside, I leaned back, resting my head against the wall, keeping my ears open. Damaged buildings like this one, with no viable space above, were largely ignored. They'd been scavenged, and scavenged again, and then left to decay like the rest of the refuse in this town.

What most didn't know about buildings like this one was that their basements went extra deep. This one had been the location of a hypertube maintenance center. There was no written record of it anywhere, at least that I'd ever found, as the building had been so badly damaged during the aftermath of the strike that no one but scavengers had noticed it.

Once I was certain all was clear, I grabbed on to the broken handrail and began my descent into the zoom tunnel that would lead me to a small maintenance shaft and the hybertube I needed.

Chapter 21

I swore under my breath as I continued to shimmy through the maintenance shaft. It was a tight fit. Tighter than I remembered, but I hadn't been down here in years.

I'd already picked my way through knee-high debris, climbed over fallen beams, belly-crawled through a labyrinth of rebar and the occasional pipes still connected at odd angles to the ceiling. I'd mountaineered over piles of bricks and tiles, all as dim light glowed from my shoulders to guide my movements.

To access the airlock, I had to drop down from the shaft. I sighed as I squeezed my body between another fallen beam and a large hunk of concrete. It was hard to imagine what I would've been doing if the world hadn't met with calamity. I certainly wouldn't be making my way through a dirty tunnel on my knees. I'd probably be working a decent job, living in a megascraper with all the bells and whistles, going about my business, my only worry about when to take my next vacation. Our ancestors had been big into vacations.

Sounded boring to me. But there was a stark difference between boring and fighting for your life every single solitary stinking day.

Something in between would've been welcome.

I knocked a piece of sheathing out of the way, finally making it to the spot where I needed to drop down onto the train. I sat, dangling my legs through the opening. A moment later, I jumped, landing with no issues, my boots making a loud echo as they hit the metal roof.

The hatch to reach the interior of the train was right under me. I knelt over the place that would've been used as an escape for passengers if there'd ever been a problem and used all my strength to unscrew the heavy steel lid. Once it was unthreaded all the way, I pulled back, bracing my knees as the fulcrum to pry it upward. It was heavy as hell. It finally eased open with a groan, and once it was up, it stayed up. I poked my head into the car to listen.

All was quiet.

I wiggled my hips through first, gripping the sides, then let go. I plunged through, dropping the two meters to the floor below. Before I did anything else, I reached over to flip a switch to defuse a small hydro-bomb concealed under a seat to my right.

Forgetting things like that would end in a messy death.

After, I placed my hands on my hips and took inventory. "I hate it down here," I muttered as I moved through the aisle. The inside of the tube had been intact when we discovered it, two seats wide on either side, each space big enough to accommodate a large male.

The chairs were appointed comfortably, with ample cushion, and covered in a synthetic fabric—red with blue circle accents. They all faced forward, the headrests thick to brace the passengers' necks. Increased acceleration took a toll on the body, so the government had tried to make the experience as comfortable as possible.

Midway through the car, the space opened up where we'd torn out the seats to create a crude sleeping area, composed of a small cot, a few raggedy blankets, and a desk with a compact radio-monitoring system. Lockland was in charge of replacing the batteries yearly.

It was a wonder he could shimmy in and out of this place, considering how hard it'd been for me. I spotted the cooling unit situated underneath the control panel and breathed a sigh of relief when I opened it up and found it still running. The energy it took to keep these things alive was minimal, thanks to the pixie motors that ran them. The protein cakes inside were extremely old and would be avoided at all costs, but there were two jugs of water and one jug of aminos if I got desperate enough.

The plan was for me to stay here for no more than a day.

Tandor's hand had been forced after he caused a scene in Port Station. The city officials would be informed. We just had to locate him and his operation, then launch our counterattack.

I sat at the small desk and flipped a switch on the board to send power to the radio receivers. Instantly, the channels lit up. A small headset lying next to the system picked up voices immediately. I placed it over my ears. I could change channels by sticking the old-fashioned jack plug into a new hole on the switchboard.

My eyebrows went up.

The voice on the other end was familiar. I stopped moving, cocking my head as my hand reached for the volume dial. "I need three rolls of micro-fiberglass," the voice said. "Delivered within the next hour."

Another voice replied, "No can do. I traded the last roll yesterday."

It was a basic conversation, except the first voice had been Case's.

There was a short pause, filled in by static, before Case responded, "Then I need five boxes of cobalt-tipped screws."

The voice replied, "I have three."

"Fine." I picked up on the irritation in his voice. "I'll be in my standard location for the next hour." Where in the hell was his standard location?

I reached for the tech phone Lockland had given me. If Case was somewhere within range, there was a good chance we could pick up his movements. It would be beneficial to keep track of him, since we knew he was planning on going after Tandor the first moment he got.

"It's Grace," I said as I depressed the button on the phone, affecting a small accent to camouflage my voice.

"Alex, here," Lockland replied.

"Channel three is active." I clicked off, allowing Lockland time to dial in. Through my headset, I could hear Case and the mystery man finalizing their rendezvous. After ten seconds, I said, "Recipient is known."

"Confirmed," Lockland said. "Will keep you posted."

Once Case was off three, I inserted the jack into various other channels, but found nothing of any interest. Lots of people talking about mundane things. I had no idea why folks spent their time listening in on conversations. Five minutes was enough to make me totally crazy.

I pushed back from the desk and walked to the far end of the tube, where the supplies were stored. The thinking was, if we were forced to retreat underground, it would be for a very serious reason, so we should have ample firepower ready to go. Kneeling, I tugged out an old aluminum container that had multiple dents in the sides and flipped up the top. To my delight, Lockland had filled it with enough compressed nano–carbon cubes to keep my Gem firing for a month.

Sliding it aside, I reached for the next box, this one made of thick graphene, and opened the lid.

"Praise you, Lockland," I said as my fingertips traced the rough contours of the hydro-bombs inside. These were midsize—pure hydrogen gas super-compressed into a rough egg form made from webbed carbon and packaged in separate padded cells. Hydro-bombs were as simple as one, two, three. One, press the arming button. Two, roll, toss, or drop on preferred target. Three, wait two seconds for the igniter to spark the gas cloud. Then, kaboom.

Each of our underground hideaways contained at least this much firepower, so I, Bender, and Lockland would be ready to move once we got confirmation about Tandor's whereabouts. The plan was to meet up and go in together, if that was possible. If not, one of us would take the lead, whoever was closest.

I went through the remaining supplies, finding some hydro-launchers and tasers. Just to pass the time, I busied myself putting together a pack. If needed, I would carry the stuff out on my back. I'd have to be extremely careful, arranging the nano-carbon cubes tightly so they couldn't bounce around.

Once I was done, I glanced around. The best course of action would be to try to get some rest. So when the call came, I'd be ready to go. I eyed the sleeping station.

With reluctance, I arranged myself on the uncomfortably hard cot, covering up with one of the blankets, which had a distinct smell of vaporized fuel and some other nasty shit. It made me think of Daze. "Dammit, kid, why'd you have to go and wreck a good thing?" I pictured his thin face and scrawny shoulders, the smears of dirt covering his cheeks, the wonder in his expression when he'd crawled into the sleeping pod, his happiness when he'd awoken. "You had so many chances. Way more than I ever had. And you blew it."

I tucked the blanket up under my arms, my weapons at the ready, my tech phone settled on my chest. I doused the light at my shoulders, leaving only the soft red glow from the radio control panel filtering through the space. I fell into a fitful sleep to the sound of mundane murmuring coming from the headset.

"Grace, it's Alex." The sound of static filled the tube. My eyes blinked open, my hand already around the phone before he could speak again. "The meet is set for one hour. Head to eight. We might be late. Message is waiting."

I depressed the button, confused as I struggled up on my elbows, my eyes blinking around the enclosure. "This is Grace. Who's going to be late?"

Late meant not coming at all.

Eight was two up from six, one of our safe houses in the canals. Basically, this meant I was going by myself, which was fine, but that wasn't according to any of the plans we'd laid yesterday. If everything had changed, Lockland should be offering some explanation for why.

I fumbled my way off the cot, untangling myself from the blanket before it tripped me, to sit at the table. I was about to pick up the headset when another missive came through. "Me and Sean. We have to attend"—static—"a meeting first."

A meeting?

That could mean only one of two things. They'd been compromised, or they wouldn't be able to arrive at eight fast enough, and Tandor was on the move, so this was our best opportunity.

"How late?" I asked.

"Very." Static. "Hit me when you're at eight."

That was it.

Lockland's abruptness was a message in and of itself. Something was up. He was warning me not to use this channel until I made it to my destination.

I pocketed the phone and shut down the power to the radio panel. Then I guzzled water out of the jug, looped my pack onto my front so I could better protect it, donned my helmet, and was up the hatch, maneuvering my shoulders through the opening, all within the span of two minutes.

The way back was slower since I was carrying sensitive supplies and I took my time. Once I reached street level, I'd be within three blocks of eight. I hadn't bothered to check my watch. I had no idea if it was daytime or blackout or how long I'd slept. I felt pretty rested, so I assumed I'd been asleep for a while, which put the time near morning.

I crept up the last flight of stairs, listening carefully

for anything out of the ordinary. Everything seemed fine as I squeezed through the sheet metal break, hoisting up my pack after I was out. I strapped it onto my back this time and made my way out the front door of the broken building.

Judging by the darkness, the sun we never saw had risen only a short time ago, meaning it was still fairly hard to see without additional light. I debated whether to traverse the streets or enter a building on the other side to access one of our protected routes via the rafters.

I chose the street, not knowing which routes Darby had babbled about to the opposition, while taking Lockland's tone to heart. The conversation had been strange, and taking one of our usual routes wouldn't be advisable.

Hurrying through the darkened streets, I avoided the wet as best I could. The rain was lighter today, rather than a solid downpour, which made it easier to move around.

It didn't take me much time to cover two blocks. Cautiously turning the corner, I spotted movement twenty meters in front of me. I ducked into a broken storefront, waiting thirty seconds before I stuck my head out.

Those were no seekers. Their movements were too precise.

They idled in front of the entryway of the building I'd planned to enter. The location was compromised. It had to be Tandor's men. I thought back to what

Lockland had said during our brief interaction. He'd mentioned attending a "meeting," which meant he wasn't coming. He'd also said there'd be a "message waiting."

We didn't leave messages. We left notes. Silicon-etched notes, to be exact.

Two more people joined the two who were already outside. Why would they be standing out in the open? Just loitering there, waiting for me to find them? Then it dawned on me that Lockland would've told them I'd be entering from above, knowing I'd come from the street. That meant that they had Lockland, and he'd been trying to warn me.

Fuck. They had Lockland.

I had enough explosives on me to blow up the entire building myself, but if Lockland was in there, I had to get him out first. He'd said both he and Bender were going to a meeting. I couldn't imagine they'd taken Bender, too, but I wasn't ruling anything out at this point.

Easing out of my position, I backtracked half a block, sticking to the shadows. Then I crossed another street, stopping in front of a broken doorway, giving the front entrance a once-over. This building wasn't one I was familiar with, which made things a little trickier. But if I could get up to the fifteenth floor, it would give me the view I needed to check things out. Our safe house was on the same story, diagonal to this out the back.

If I'd come in from our protected route, like Lockland told them, I would've come from the building behind it, not this one. So, technically, they shouldn't be monitoring it.

I wouldn't know until I entered.

Taking a deep breath, I stepped over the threshold.

Chapter 22

The first few floors were quiet. I'd slowly and laboriously sidestepped my way through the junk and litter, moving as stealthily as I could. Judging by the amount of heaped wreckage, scattered every which way, this building wasn't in use.

Chalk one up for the good guys.

With trepidation, I'd switched off all my tech phones. Lockland had specified one hour for rendezvous, which would be coming up in about five to ten minutes, going by my internal clock. When I didn't show up at the agreed-upon time, he would be forced to reach out again. I couldn't risk any of Tandor's goons hearing my phones go off. Once I was sure I was alone, I'd turn them on again.

As I rounded the thirteenth story, something rattled from above. Luckily for me, there was no door separating the stairwell and the landing. Ducking into a hallway, I braced myself against the wall, listening. Distinct movements came from overhead.

Someone was up there.

Damn. That wasn't the scenario I'd hoped for.

This floor was only two away from my destination. There was a possibility I could scout the building next door from here. I turned and made my way down a long hallway, stepping over a bunch of broken hologram cameras, marked by their distinct logo, which were two hands joined inside the shadow of a projection light.

Before the dark days, hologram technology had been advanced. If both parties owned the basic elements, a trio of triangulated cameras, and an ultrafast com-connection, you could project your image cleanly and interact with the other person. From what I'd read, the experience had been pretty lifelike. Very few hologram cameras survived the catastrophic events, and the technology to build them had died with the meteor. I'd heard rumblings that the government had access to a few, but nothing had been circumstantiated.

I was surprised to see some of the garbage strewn around intact. Meaning it was broken, but pieces were salvageable. By all rights, this building should've been picked over a long time ago. I made a mental note to check back here after life went back to normal.

Because, you know, thinking life wouldn't go back to normal was not an option.

At the end, rain and wind met me head on. I entered the office on the left, which would give me the best viewing angle. With luck, I could spot something. Two strides before the exposed wall, I dropped to my knees, using my hands to clear a path, crawling toward the opening, moving as quietly as I could.

The sky hadn't lightened much, even though morning was creeping in. Anyone scouring the area from above with infrared goggles or a decent visor could potentially pick up my heat signature. If Tandor was smart, he'd have lookouts arrayed at varying intervals inside the building to monitor the surrounding areas. But it was hard to actually know how smart this zealot was, as he'd already made a bunch of stumbles. If he was confident that Lockland had been telling the truth, and I was going to come through a known path, he may have let his guard down.

I stopped a few paces from the edge, ducking behind a pile of debris consisting of a broken chair, disintegrated ceiling tiles, and part of a metal cabinet of some kind, doing my best to keep my body mass to a bare minimum.

My gaze swept left to right, starting at the lowest floor, swiveling back and forth. As I tilted my head up, something caught my eye.

Two red heat spots around the location of our safe room. The question was, was Lockland in there, or was he somewhere else? It would've been too coincidental for Tandor to have his operations in that building all along.

I swore under my breath as I backed away. In the

hallway, I weighed my options, leaning against the wall out of the rain. I could try to infiltrate the building next door, do some damage, free Lockland, and in the process take out some of Tandor's followers. Or I could lie low and wait for them to give up on me and then follow them out.

Both had their merits.

If I attacked, I put Tandor on the defense and made him careless. If I followed, I could end this once and for all.

Follow, it was.

Resigned to my decision, I picked my way back toward the stairwell, trying to avoid making any sound. At the doorway, I leaned my shoulder against the wall, listening. A quiet pattering of noise echoed downward.

Footfalls on the stairs.

One person.

It wasn't a seeker, because the steps were too even and measured. And judging from the quick pace, whoever it was had no idea I was here. If they'd suspected anyone was in the building, they wouldn't be stepping half that fast.

I inched closer, easing off my pack and setting it to the side.

When the footfalls hit the landing beside me, I grabbed on to the doorjamb, cocking my wrists, using my upper strength to propel my body, leading with my legs, an elbow firmly tucked into my ribs to keep me rotating cleanly.

My boots connected squarely with a sturdy chest.

A loud *oof* followed as what appeared to be a male of average height and build flew backward. The momentum continued to spin me once I hit the ground, but I recovered quickly, jamming a knee into his trachea. The force of my kick had sent him crashing back into the stairs. His un-helmeted head had hit first. One of his arms was at an odd angle.

He was out cold.

I whipped out my Gem and my taser, aiming them at his lifeless body, just to be on the safe side. After all, he could wake up.

The man was unfamiliar to me, but I had no idea if he was one of Tandor's or someone else minding his own business. All I knew was that he was down, he had short black hair, his chromes were askew, one covering the top of one cheekbone, the other haphazardly settled over one eye, and he was going to have a roaring headache when he woke.

Another noise sounded from above. My hips shifted as my arms came up, both my weapons extending out in front of me, aimed at the new threat, my knee still pinning the guy beneath me.

The figure at the top of the landing raised his hands in the face of my firepower. He had on a dark helmet, the visor down.

But I'd know that trench anywhere.

I lowered my taser, but not my Gem. "What the fuck, Case? What are you doing here?"

"I could ask you the same thing."

"Who's this guy?" I asked.

"My source," he said. "If he's still alive."

I stepped off the man, keeping my Gem trained in front of me. "He's alive, but he's not going to feel so hot when he wakes up. Should've had a helmet on."

Case crossed his arms, staying where he was on the landing. "He just explained that they're planning your demise next door."

"I figured as much. Is Tandor over there?" I asked, my voice hopeful.

"Nope."

I backed away from the crumpled man. "Do you know where he is?"

Case came forward. When I didn't rebuff his movements, he eased down a few steps. "Not at the moment." He stopped next to the man, squatting as he laid two fingers over his throat. When he was satisfied the guy still had a pulse, he stood.

"They're holding at least one of my friends."

Grunting a noncommittal response, Case continued down to the landing. I appraised him. Going by only what I could see, which wasn't much, I'd say he still looked tired. "What's your plan?" he asked.

"That depends. If my friend's next door, I'll break him out and kill everyone in my way. If not, I wait until they know I'm not showing and follow them. They'll eventually lead me to Tandor."

"Your friend is not next door."

I narrowed my gaze. "Then where the hell is he?"

"I don't know, but I was about to find out." He

gestured to the man on the stairs. "He was going to report back in ten minutes."

I shrugged, my gun unwavering. "Not my issue. How'd you know they would be in the building next door?"

Again, Case gestured to the unconscious man.

"What did he say about me?"

"Not much. Your reputation is serving you well. They're being cautious."

I snorted. "Cautious? They had guys milling around on the street and multiple bodies in the building. This is a rookie operation."

Case flipped his visor up, his gray eyes boring into mine. "They don't have just one of your guys, they have two, and the big guy is pissed as hell. It's not so amateur when they manage to take them both down without causing a commotion. They knew where to find them, and they picked them up easily."

I wasn't going to give Case the satisfaction of showing even the smallest hint of a reaction that they had Bender. And he was right, that meant the operation wasn't so rookie after all. My brain was already processing the next plan. "This is where we part ways," I said, my voice even.

"No. This is where we help each other," Case corrected. "I'm guessing you have ammunition with you. You have the means, and I have locations."

I shook my head. "Helping is not my style."

Case tapped on a shoulder light and tugged off his helmet, his hair sticking up. "Your friends aren't next door. They're north with Tandor and the rest of his guys. How are you going to get there without a craft? And how are you planning on penetrating a heavily guarded compound without help? Tandor is intelligent and persistent, even though he's made mistakes, and your crew is tied up at the moment. I'm all you've got."

He was right.

If Tandor's men jumped into a craft, I'd be back to square one, unable to help my friends. Not having access to Luce was a problem. With my Gem still aimed at Case's chest, my eyes on his, I fished out my tech phone. They'd be expecting me to check in. I could keep up the charade as long as it took. "It's Grace," I said into the speaker. "Change of plans. Can't meet at eight. Need a new location."

Static came over the line. Then, finally, "Twenty-se—" Lockland's voice was cut off abruptly.

Twenty-seven was our phrase for north.

Dammit. Case was telling the truth. He knew where they were. I had to make a choice. I lowered my Gem and ducked into the hallway, plucking up my pack and shouldering it as I headed toward the office I'd just occupied. I ducked behind the pile once again, scanning for movement.

The heat signatures were already gone.

A moment later, dronecraft props sounded from above. I watched four of them take off from the top floor.

Once they'd vanished, I turned to Case, who was silhouetted in the doorway. "Where's Seven parked?"

Chapter 23

Case had parked his craft close by, hidden underneath a bunch of broken rafters, undetectable from above.

"Head two blocks south, one block west," I directed once we were in the air.

"South is not north."

"No shit. But we need more supplies. The stuff in my pack will do damage, but if we want to bring down the house, we're going to need more." Swinging by my residence in the canal was risky, as I had no idea if Tandor and his crew knew about it via Darby and would be keeping tabs on it. But I'd know instantly if my security had been breached, even from a distance.

Case did as I asked.

I fished my chromes out of my pocket and flipped my visor, donning them, clicking the dial to ultraviolet. "Land on the building up ahead." I gestured out the windshield. "The one with the forked antenna and four rafters that look like fingers. If you can do it without lights, all the better. The roof is clean, plenty of places to choose from." Case clicked off his running lights five meters away and set down with no issues. "Stay here," I ordered, popping the door.

We were on top of the building next to mine. I'd set up a small lookout enclosure, made out of sheet metal, for times like these. Emergency times. Times when my residence might be under attack. Once there, I moved the necessary pieces of sheeting away and crouched at the edge, scanning my tarps and panels, clicking through my chromes. "Fuck."

"What?"

Without taking my eyes off the scene, I said, "I thought I told you to stay in the craft."

"I was bored."

I snorted. On my roof next door, two of my devices had gone off, doing minimal damage to the surrounding area. Thankfully, nobody had tried to open the hatch. If they had, the entire roof would've blown sky high. Some of my tarps had been adjusted, so that wasn't good news. From this angle, I could also see onto my garden balcony. Nothing seemed amiss. "Stay here. I have to go check something." I made a move to push past him, but Case's hands stilled me, gripping the tops of my forearms. I whipped my arms away, giving him a look like I'd make him hurt if he didn't let me go. He backed off as I moved away.

He followed. "I can help."

"I don't need your help."

"That may be true, but we're running out of time. Once those guys return to the compound, Tandor's going to have to make some decisions, and my guess is it will involve bodily harm to your friends." I walked toward the stairwell that would take me down four stories. Case kept dogging me. "They'll make contact via your phone, which they already know you're listening to. They'll give you a time and location. If you fail to meet it, they will kill one, and then the other. We need to make it north before they do. They won't be expecting us to arrive ahead of them."

Case was right. On all counts.

Tandor would most certainly use my friends to get to me. If he threatened their lives, I'd have no choice but to acquiesce to his terms. But what Tandor didn't know was that I had enough bombs and precision equipment to take him out at a hefty distance. "Fine," I said, not bothering to turn around, "but keep up."

I removed my chromes, stuffing them into my vest as I entered the stairwell. This building was taller than mine, but its internal structure was near breaking point. All one had to do was listen to the noises it made in the wind to know it was unstable. It creaked and groaned like an ornery grandfather.

I hadn't needed to use this surveillance point in years, which was a good thing.

Case trailed after me. "This building sounds like it's going to collapse any moment."

"It very well might, but it's hung on this long."

"So, why are we here?"

Down four flights, I stopped at a closed door, glancing over my shoulder. "Because we need to be." Placing my hand on the knob, I jiggled it. The locking mechanism rattled. I took a stiff pallidum wire out of a pocket and jammed it into the hole I'd drilled above the knob. The lock sprang effortlessly. This kind of barrier wouldn't keep out anyone but a seeker.

Opening the door, I cocked my head to listen, because it was necessary. Other than all the menacing creaking, it was clear.

Once upon a time, this building had been apartments, just like mine next door, but not as nice. I headed down to the end of the hall and shouldered open another door. This unit had most of its walls covered in viewing screens, which were all broken or cracked, with pieces littering the floor. We crunched over the shards, making our way toward the integrated balcony. Each apartment here had its own balcony, unlike my building, which had one per floor.

I stuck my hand out to keep Case back. "We look first, then enter."

He inclined his head. The wind breezed through the broken glass that used to separate the unit from the garden, causing the metal cable swing bang against the outer wall.

I scanned the balcony, detecting no movement or heat signature across the way. Edging out, I took hold of the cable. "We're riding this over"—I jutted my shoulder toward my building—"to there." Case didn't reply, which was smart. This particular swing was attached to the roof of the unit two balconies up, hooked here to provide a ride straight across to my residence. There was very little room to get momentum in this small space, so if you sucked riding one, you'd thump back against the building. "If you're not game, I'll go by myself."

"I didn't say I wasn't game."

"You didn't need to," I responded wryly. "Your voice said it all when it broke there at the end. I'm not sure why everyone hates swings. They're a great way to get around. Quiet and efficient."

"And deadly."

"Only if you do it wrong."

"Or if they're not secured properly."

I turned around to peer at him through my lowered visor. Lots of body heat reflected back. "Are you questioning my engineering skills?"

"We met two days ago."

"You had no problem letting me fly your craft, and you've been following me around and taking my orders thus far. Why doubt me now?" I jumped up on the railing. This swing was fitted with a foot loop.

"Where exactly are we headed?" Case asked.

"None of your business, and if you're smart, you'll erase this location from your memory completely. The next time you come back, if you're brave enough to try, there'll be a number of traps in place from the roof to here that will blow you up."

"I'm not a burglar." His voice held resentment.

"We only met two days ago."

He grumbled, but said nothing.

"Watch what I do, and copy me exactly. Once I'm there, I'll have my supplies together in less than three minutes. The one thing you have to remember is to hold on to the cable once you land, so we have a way to get back." When he didn't answer, I glanced behind me, inserting my foot into the loop. "If you're not up for this, go upstairs and wait for me in the craft."

"If I go with you, can we bring more?"

"Obviously. I only have one back and two arms. If you come, we have two backs and four arms." I'd left my other pack in Case's clean backseat. He nodded. I took that as he was coming along. I didn't care either way. I jumped, shifting my body forward to force the pendulum to swing as quickly as I could.

The distance between the buildings was only about six meters. When I was within a meter of my balcony wall, I bowed my back, clearing the railing, keeping a hand gripped loosely around the cable, allowing my gloves to slide. I landed smoothly, even though I hadn't used the swing since I'd set it up. The rope wanted to snap back, but I held firmly.

I turned, giving Case a thumbs-up, walking back a few paces before flinging the cable toward him. Even if he missed, it would bounce back to him eventually, since it was secured at the front of the building, not hanging over the side of it.

He caught it on the first try.

I wasn't going to stick around to watch him cross. I had things to do. I'd switched my E-unit off when

Darby and I had left, not knowing when I'd be back. I popped open the top. My nano-carbon cubes were right where I'd left them.

I walked around the back. I hadn't showed Darby where I stored my cache of all hydro-related things, which in hindsight was a good thing. I was still in disbelief that the government had him. I couldn't think about that now. After we took care of Tandor, Darby was next on the list.

Crouching, I eased back a partition I'd made in the wall and dragged out a large box, being extra careful to slide it slowly, making sure it didn't bump against anything. Behind me there was a thump, followed by a short gasp. Case's feet landed right where they needed to be. It was impressive he'd made it on his first try.

"Where should I tie this up?" he asked casually.

I motioned toward the side where I'd hammered a double-sided hook into the wall. "Wrap it there. Make sure it's secure."

Once Case was done, he came around the machine where I was carefully placing hydro-bombs the size of my fist inside two protective foam carrying cases.

When they were full, I clicked them shut and slipped them into two glycine-fiber duffels. Twenty would be more than enough firepower to blow a compound sky high.

"A hydro-grenade launcher is hard to come by," Case said as I tied the tube onto the top of the duffel closest to me with steel micro-strand yarn. The launcher was as long as my forearm.

"Yep." When I'd gathered all the gear, I slid the big box, still packed with bombs, back into its safe place and shut it up tight. "I'm not sure if you have a laser, like my Gem, but if you do, and it takes nano-carbon cube ammunition, I have some. Look in there." I bobbed my head toward the end of the E-unit. Case followed my gaze and walked over and lifted the lid. His eyes met mine over the short span of the machine. I could tell he was impressed, but not by how much. After all, his own arsenal could put mine to shame. He scooped out a handful. "You might want to be careful with those," I said. "They're handmade and therefore unstable. I've never had an issue, but they could very well blow up in your face."

He reached into his coat and pulled out a magnetic pulse gun, which shot a high-energy pulse that excited the molecules of whatever it hit, causing the victim to basically turn to liquid internally. "I don't have a laser, but I have this." He held it up. "And it happens to use nano-carbon cubes."

I flipped on my shoulder light as I stood, watching as he filled the cubes one by one into the magazine. "I've only seen two of those guns before." I made my way around the unit, fitting one duffel over one shoulder and holding the other. "If they hit their mark, it can be pretty gruesome. I've heard they're not all that accurate."

"They are when I shoot."

I didn't respond. Having something that Case needed, like fuel, made everything more complicated.

He might have his own cubes, but more was always better. I was going to have to think about ways to protect this place adequately in the future. I'd given him no hint this was my residence. For all he knew, this was just one of my many stashes. I thrust the duffel in my hand at him. "Here, take this. Don't bump into anything. There are ten hydro-bombs inside." I continued over to the cable, unhooking it and climbing onto a pedestal I'd made that was welded to the ground. I inserted my foot into the loop. "I'll see you on the other side," I told him. "If you don't make it, I'm taking your craft, no hard feelings."

Then I arched back and propelled myself forward.

Chapter 24

The moment Case lifted Seven up in the air, my tech phone went off. It wasn't the new one Lockland had given me. It was my old one, on our regular channel. My hopes lifted. Maybe Case had been wrong, and Bender hadn't been taken and was contacting me.

They were dashed a second later when a voice came over the line as I drew it out of my pocket. It wasn't familiar, but they knew my handle. "Ella. Come in, Ella."

I glanced at Case to see if he recognized the voice. He shook his head.

"I'm not answering." I stuffed it back in my vest. "Once I hear his instructions, the clock starts ticking."

Case increased the throttle, and the info screen blinked fifty kilometers per hour.

A few moments later, static buzzed out of the black phone Lockland had given me. Once again, the correct handle was called out. This time, it was Lockland's voice. "Grace, it's Alex." Static. "I know you're monitoring." More static. "The meet is set for thirty minutes. Go where you picked up the kid." The phone abruptly shut off, no static, just dead air.

That meant they'd turned it completely off, not caring if I got the message or not. I addressed Case. "Can they get from their holding place in The North to the gorge in thirty?"

"They're likely already there." Case gained altitude, turning the craft to head toward the cliff where I'd first met Daze.

"What do you mean?" I sat up straighter in my seat. "They were just in the canals waiting to ambush me, and you said they were heading north to where Tandor was holed up."

He shrugged. "They must've changed their plan. I don't know everything."

"My craft is in Port Station. So how do they know I can get to the gorge so quickly?" I drew my Gem and locked it against his temple. "Care to answer that?"

Case gritted his teeth. "I had no reason to let them know."

"Bullshit. You want Tandor dead, but you could care less if it comes at a cost to me or my friends. Admit it. You somehow orchestrated all this. What? Did you leave something with the guy on the steps? A note that I was with you?" I swore. I hadn't bothered to pat the guy down or search his pockets before we left. How many times could I be duped in a week? The jury was out. The number might possibly be infinite.

"Don't fuck with me, Case. I will blow your brains out and take your craft."

"I have a plan."

"Keep talking." At the speed Case was going, we'd be at the gorge with time to spare. I reached to a hidden pocket inside my vest and withdrew a small dart, palming it.

"My snitch compromised me. It was the only way."

"So you waited conveniently in the building next door, because unlike Tandor and his men, you knew I wouldn't be stupid enough to blindly follow Lockland's directives without checking it out first? Your insider was coming to make sure you paid up?"

"Something like that."

"Everything like that. What did you promise them?" He turned to glance my way, but the Gem was pressed firmly into his face, the cold barrel leaving an indent. "Keep your eyes on the horizon. We have a date to keep. What did you tell them? I want everything, so spill." My voice was calm and steady.

"I have a plan."

"I don't give a shit about your plan. We're doing this my way. What did you promise them? And this is the last time I'm asking."

"That I'd deliver you at the appropriate time and place."

"Am I alive in this scenario? Awake? Unconscious? Armed with enough bombs to blow up the goddamn gorge? You forgot to tell them that part, or maybe you just didn't have time? What do you get in return?"

"Tandor."

"It's not just Tandor, is it? There has to be more. You knew I had enough firepower to take him out. What's worth my life and the lives of my friends?"

The ground beneath us gave way to a sea of broken trees, the gnarled tops speeding by in a dark blur of beckoning fingers. "My sister." I didn't respond. Instead, I slid my gun next to his ear. "She's one of his followers."

"I don't give a fuck."

"I know."

"I'm not trading my family for yours."

"I know."

"Here's what's going to happen," I relayed carefully. "You're going to follow my instructions to a T. If you don't, you're dead. Up ahead, I want you to drop altitude, skim the surface of that old vehicle road below us. We're going to be setting down in a couple of kilometers. I know a back way in." I'd been out to the gorge countless times before. If anything, this location was to my advantage. I wondered if Lockland or Bender had something to do with that. "I know you don't have a scrambler on this, or you would've used it the first time you tried to track me, so we're going to have to go old school and fly low, staying out of sight." I refrained from kicking the shit out of his dash. Having Luce right now would have been a godsend.

"I wasn't going to sell you out," he tried. "We have enough firepower to take them down." His movements were stiff and jerky, his tone raspy, layered with a hint of desperation.

"*I* have enough firepower," I corrected. "And you had no idea what I would be able to get my hands on before you sold me out."

"I knew."

"How? Did you scout out my balcony all on your own? See my E-unit from a building you've never been in before?"

"You have a reputation, and in the bunker, you hinted at being able to round up a lot of firepower."

"I do have a reputation, and you should've paid more attention. Now it's going to cost you." He tried to move his head again, but my arm was locked. "If you do as I say, I won't kill you, even though that's my inclination at the moment." He dropped altitude easily, positioning Seven above the road I'd indicated, out of sight from eyes in the sky. "Very soon, there will be an opening on your left. It's a leftover clearing from when people used utility poles, but wide enough to fly through. Take it."

Case made the turn effortlessly. He was an excellent pilot, but he'd never hear it from me. "You're making a mistake if you don't hear me out," he said. "This is the only chance we're going to get. We have to work together."

"Wrong. I've made plenty of mistakes in the past few days, but working with you won't be one of them." In this location, we were only a few kilometers away from the gorge. "If Tandor's smart, he'll have scouts positioned in the air and on the ground from here on in. What kind of tracking monitors does this thing have? I haven't seen any blinking lights."

Case flipped two unmarked switches. "When we get within three kilometers of another craft, a beep will sound." As if on cue, the thing beeped.

One lonely beep.

"Does it sound more than once if there's more than one craft?"

"No."

"Helpful." Clearly, the Q7 was meant for speed and not much else. "Up ahead, set her down when you see even ground." There was another alert. "Does the beep give us any information other than distance?"

"Nope."

My hand absently stroked the dart I had concealed. I'd been wrestling with the fact that Tandor had known where to find Lockland and Bender. Our underground safe houses should've been more than secure. Even if Darby had babbled, he wouldn't have had all the exact locations. I narrowed my gaze, suddenly understanding. "Where'd you put it?"

"What?"

"The tracker. And how'd you get it on me without my knowing? I'm assuming it has a listening component and that's how you knew our movements." While I'd been jamming his craft, thinking I had everything under control, he'd placed a tracker on me.

"In the back of your hand."

My eyebrows rose. "Did you say *in*?"

"You were sedated with gas in the sleeping pod."

"Which hand?"

"Right."

I slid the dart under my thigh. "Land the craft." I gestured toward an opening coming up on the left. "Then shut it off."

Case complied. A few beeps went off, so there were crafts within three kilometers of us, but this spot was sufficiently concealed from the main route. Tandor, coming up from the South, would likely not know all the ins and outs of this area, especially since it was a sprawling wasteland.

I lifted my Gem a few centimeters off his face and allowed Case to turn. "This wasn't how this was supposed to go." His gray eyes held emotion I couldn't name and didn't care about.

"This was exactly how it was supposed to go. You captured me in Port Station, forced me back to your bunker, knowing you'd exchange me later for your sister. You sedated me, injected a tracker, spilled all our movements to the guy you're trying to kill, convinced him you were on his side, all while planning to double-cross him and get your revenge. Listen, Case, I get it. I don't really blame you. I might've done something similar if I were in your shoes, especially if I was out for blood. But what you did makes us enemies, not allies." I gave him a look as I held up my right hand. "Where is it?"

Case indicated to the soft place between my index finger and my middle finger.

Military trackers, which I assumed was what he used, could be as tiny as a grain of sand. They were injected via a thin needle, painless and virtually undetectable.

"We can still work togeth—"

I fisted the dart. "No, we really can't." I brought it forward, whizzing my hand down, slamming the nose of it into the top of his leg.

I watched his expression as he realized what I'd done.

It wasn't as shocked as it could've been.

A few seconds later, his eyes began to blink rapidly, before beginning to slide shut. I leaned over and whispered into his ear, "You're not the only one who knows how to put people to sleep. Oh, and once you wake up, get the fuck out of here. If I see you again, you're a dead man."

He slumped toward me, and I pushed him the opposite direction, using a little extra force to get the job done. He hit his door with a loud thunk and stayed there.

I'd given him the biggest dart I had, one of three I carried on me. He was six-three or six-four and all brawn, but the dose I'd given him should be sufficient to keep him out for about an hour. Plenty of time to achieve my many goals.

But first things first.

I set my Gem down and unclipped a knife strapped to my thigh, balancing it on my leg. Then I plucked a small vial out of my vest and popped the cork with my teeth. Picking up my knife, the blade thin and ridiculously sharp, I inserted the tip into the flesh were Case had indicated. As blood began to flow, I collected it in the open vial. When I was satisfied enough had gone in, I dug out my chromes and put them on.

I switched to ultraviolet as I shook the vial.

Sure enough, a pink dot flashed in the sea of red. "Bastard," I muttered, turning to examine Case's slumped form against the door. "I should probably amend that to *tricky bastard.*" As far as I knew, I'd never been sedated without my knowledge.

I had, however, had tracking devices injected into me at various times in my life.

Sheathing my knife back on my thigh, I took a medi-towel from my pocket. I bit the package open with my teeth, and once the blood had been absorbed and the cut sufficiently clotted, I reached into his much-too-clean backseat and grabbed the duffel with the rocket launcher tied to it and my pack from the hypertube. I had no choice but to leave the other duffel here, as I had no more body parts to carry anything. Then I popped my door and got out. I was going to have to race to make the deadline.

Once the pack was firmly strapped to my front and the duffel slung over my shoulder, I began to jog, keeping a slow, even gait, my arms holding everything stable. I'd come in from this direction only one other time, but that's all I needed. The sky had brightened and the drizzle was cooperating.

As I ran, I planned my attack.

Chapter 25

I lobbed the mic chip, the size of a pebble, into the trees to my right, then immediately circled left, keeping low. The device had a range of about twenty meters.

Using my index finger as I jogged, I adjusted the earpiece, immediately picking up quiet murmuring. The group was situated where I'd saved Daze from plunging to his death only days before—correction, *thought* I'd saved him.

I spotted bits of movement through the trees as I picked my way toward my best advantage point, but I couldn't see much.

"She should be here by now," a male voice declared.

"I told you not to trust him," another voice countered, irritated. "He has no loyalty to us."

I snorted softly. "Case has no loyalty to anyone. Should've figured that out long before this, dummy."

"He'll bring her." I straightened. This particular

voice was strong and regulated. It had to be Tandor, or at the very least, someone in charge.

A strange noise erupted in my ear, which I quickly realized was propellers. A craft was landing in the area. Shouting sounded before the fans died down. I heard a door open and close. "No sign of them," a male voice declared, along with loud, crunching footsteps. He must be closest to the mic chip.

"What about readings from other crafts in the area?" the strong voice in charge asked.

"I told you she wouldn't come." Lockland!

"Shut the fuck up." There was the sound of a fist striking flesh, followed by, "*Ooof.*"

Dammit.

"We'll give them five more minutes," the leader said. "Then we depart."

"Then what?" a voice asked in an irritated whine, this one distinctly female. "You said she has the key we need. How are we going to get it?"

What key?

"We'll find a way to get it, one way or another."

"What are we going to do with this lot, then?" another male voice asked.

I was listening hard, leaning forward, my head cocked in their direction, wishing I could see what was taking place.

"We toss them over the side. If she doesn't come now, they're no good to us anymore," the voice I was coming to know as Tandor stated with harsh cruelty.

"If she gets away, she'll go to ground and we won't

be able to find her," a new male voice said. By my count, there were at least six present, likely more loitering around. "The outskirt told us he wasn't able to inject her with the tracker we gave him, and their inner network is tricky, as we've already seen." So Case had lied to them about the tracker, feeding them only what he wanted them to know.

It didn't make his treachery any less infuriating.

"We got what we needed with the last of the Babble," Tandor said. "We know where she lives. We can, and will, track her down. She'll have to come up for air sometime. We can wait her out."

His cocky and self-assured attitude pissed me off. He thought he had the upper hand. And no, he couldn't wait me out, because he wasn't going to have to.

It was time to move.

I slid my packs onto the ground as quietly as I could, unzipping them, taking out the hydro-bombs, and untying the launcher.

First things first.

I filled my Gem with nano-carbon cubes. This would be my primary weapon when I arrived at the clearing. Then I emptied my pockets of nonessentials and refilled them with egg-sized mini-bombs, leaving the larger, fist-sized bombs for the front two pockets.

Once I was ready, I moved forward, low to the ground, launcher in hand, leaving my packs behind, dodging between tree trunks. I had to get a good look at what was going on before I sent any bombs flying. I didn't want to put my friends in jeopardy.

Another craft flew into the area.

I couldn't quite see it, but judging by the loudness in my earpiece, it was just up ahead. I had to wait until they turned the props off to hear what they were saying.

"No sign of her or the other craft," a new voice announced.

Creeping ever closer, I veered to the right. In the distance, I could finally spot a craft through the battered tree trunks, the voices getting clearer with every step I took closer to the mic.

"She's not coming," the female voice said. "If she did something to my brother—"

"Shut up, Carmen. Your piece of shit brother was never going to help us anyway," a male voice with a hint of a lisp said. "We never should've trusted him. After you killed Frankie, he wrote you off."

"Frankie had it coming," Carmen whined.

"Nice thing to say," another voice grunted. "He was your kid."

"You don't know anything—"

Tandor cut her off. "Toss these two over the side, and this one." I heard a shallow squeak. Daze?

I had a clear shot at the craft. It was a good place as any to start. The only thing I wasn't sure of was how close everyone was to it. I craned my neck, arching my back to get a better vantage point.

Then I saw them.

Bender and Lockland were kneeling at the very edge of the cliff, blindfolded, their hands tied behind their backs. Someone was walking toward them.

Time to act.

I set the rocket launcher down and scooped two of the eggs out of my pockets. I stood and tossed them, one after the other, as far as I could toward the parked craft. Couldn't risk shooting off the bigger bomb with the launcher at the moment, as the blast might toss my friends over the side of the cliff. I was glad I'd sighted their location before I decided on what to use.

By the time the explosions hit, I was already running.

The intensity of the bombs came through my earpiece, and I cursed. I hadn't remembered to take the damn thing out. With one hand, I grabbed another egg, and with the other, I ripped it from my ear and tossed it away.

Up ahead was chaos. Everyone was running.

Shouts of alarm sounded in every direction, many of Tandor's followers drawing their weapons and aiming them back at the craft, like I'd intended.

"You have to find me first, motherfuckers," I muttered as I tossed another egg and then another, arcing them as far away from me as I could as I raced forward, veering toward the gorge.

I gathered a handful of nano-carbon cubes and unholstered my Gem, bursting into the clearing, my gun trained on the one I was certain was Tandor, who was uncomfortably close to Bender. My other hand swung, letting the cubes fly, flinging them as hard as I could at the ground in front of the folks who had turned their attention toward me.

They went off in a series of short blasts around those who were closest.

If I stopped my momentum, it was all over. There were too many. I needed to keep the chaos going.

My hand found another egg, and just as my fingers encircled it, I slid, going down on a thigh, yelling, "One meter forward and to your left."

Bender lunged immediately, jamming his shoulder to the left. I watched in satisfaction as Tandor stumbled.

I came to a stop in front of Lockland, spinning at the last moment, squeezing the trigger of my gun into the crowd. I made the most of it, slicing the white-hot laser in front of me with a wave of my arm, hitting five at once, while instructing Lockland, "No room behind!"

Lockland rolled forward, bringing his arms up under him as he went, ripping his blindfold off as he stood. I jumped up and placed an egg in his tethered hands.

Before Lockland could toss it, or I could get off another blast, a commanding voice yelled, "Stop, or he dies." The words cut through the chaos as efficiently as a diamond blade through stone.

My hands were still extended, my gun trained on the new group that had amassed in front of us. Tandor had to have at least forty men here, fifteen to twenty of whom were already down.

I angled my head toward the voice, not lowering my hand, fiercely hoping that Bender had gotten free and Tandor was down, not the other way around.

That wasn't the case. Not even a little bit.

Bender's blindfold was off, but he hadn't gained the upper hand. In fact, Tandor's large gun was crammed into his neck. It was a wicked-looking laser gun, twice as big as my Gem. But that wasn't the only thing that could kill him. Bender knelt, facing me, his legs precariously hanging over the cliff's edge. One slight movement and Tandor could send him tumbling to his death.

"Now that I have your attention, let's talk." Tandor's cadence was easy, but I spotted a small tic strumming at his jawline. It was the only thing belying his smooth, unflustered projection. He was rattled. Good. I didn't know what I'd expected, but he was a fairly ordinary-looking guy with a bland face, thin frame, and no defining features. He seemed like the kind of guy who holed up in his residence and hoarded his resources, refusing to help others.

In other words, a meek asshole.

There was a flicker of movement behind Tandor. I squinted as Daze stepped out from his shadow, stumbling as he went. It was clear that Daze hadn't chosen to reveal himself willingly, as Tandor had a firm grip around his neck.

The kid looked ragged.

Bruises and dried blood covered his face and hands, the only things visible at the moment. Judging by his wincing, his body was battered as well. His face was streaked with lines of smeared dirt, tracking from his eyes down to his chin. It was puzzling to me why they'd hurt him. Hadn't he done as they asked? Case said that he'd been caught stealing. So what? Everybody stole around here to survive.

After giving Daze a once-over, my eyes traced to the man who held him, the grasp obviously painful from the look on the kid's face. Tandor was waiting for my reply. "I'm just warning you, I'm not in a very chatty mood," I said.

All I needed was a distraction to get him to step away from the two of them.

A single distraction.

"Drop your weapon," Tandor instructed. When I didn't move to comply, he pressed the barrel of his gun deeper into Bender's neck, causing Bender's body to teeter backward. "It's not going to take me much to finish him off. Do as I say. And you"—he nodded toward Lockland—"get down on your knees."

Reluctantly, I squatted, placing my gun on the ground in front of me as Lockland knelt. He hadn't told Lockland to get rid of the bomb in his hand, so I assumed he hadn't seen me give it to him. That would come in handy. I hoped sooner rather than later. "It's down," I said. "Tell me what you want."

A malicious grin full of ugly teeth spread over Tandor's face, like getting me to comply had been ridiculously easy. I ignored him. Instead, I raked my gaze over the area, searching for the advantage. I knew what to look for, and I was confident I'd find it.

Plus, Tandor had no idea what I had in my pockets, and his jaw was doing that tic thing.

"I want the key," he demanded. "If you hand it to me right now, I'll let you and your friends go."

What fucking key? was what I wanted to say. And bullshit. He would kill us all where we stood as soon as he got this mysterious prize.

I had to play this right, even though belligerently sticking up both my middle fingers and telling him to fuck off sounded appealing. "I don't have your key," I said, my voice even. "Now that that's settled, feel free to let me and my friends go." My voice ended on pissy.

Apparently, belligerent was part of my molecular chemistry.

"You lied." His tone was like ice as he turned his attention on Daze, backhanding the kid so hard he fell to the ground. Daze's palms scraped the rocks, and a new line of blood opened up on his forehead.

"Hey—" I was angry, and my voice echoed it. I took a step forward without realizing it.

Tandor leaned into Bender once again, and I stopped instantly.

Another shit-eating grin spread over Tandor's face. He was enjoying this immensely. Shelling out pain to others. It's what he lived for. "Tell her what you did." Tandor addressed Daze, who was still on all fours.

The kid didn't lift his gaze, his head so low I had trouble hearing him. "I stole something. Then I gave it to you."

He was talking about the quantum drive.

The key was the drive. Why in the hell didn't he just call it a drive?

I played dumb. "No, you didn't," I answered, my voice firm. "I would've remembered a key. Maybe you dropped it over the gorge accidentally?"

"He's not talking about something shaped like a *key*." Tandor was creeping toward furious, a vein pulsing like it was running for its life on his forehead. "He took something from me, something extremely valuable, and I want it back."

"*Hm*," I hedged. "You're not talking about the quantum drive, are you? Because I thought that was just a ploy to get me to go after the pico so you could kill me, then get on with your nefarious plans to take over the government. I must not have all the facts straight." I was one step away from crossing my arms, but then Daze lifted his head.

The kid was scared, his expression hollow, his eyes wild.

At that moment, Tandor lifted a boot and lodged it firmly into Daze's stomach. It took every inch of control I had not to react. The urchin grunted and rolled with the force of the kick, wrapping his skinny arms tightly around his middle, tears leaking down his face, his lungs gasping for air.

My fingers curled into fists. If I let on that I cared about this kid, Tandor would gain more leverage.

"Tell her!" Tandor roared, his focus firmly on Daze.

I was forced to amend my first impression of this monster. Outwardly, he came off as a mundane asshole. But Tandor wasn't a guy who holed up in his residence and hoarded his goods. He was the worst sort of human. One who took greedy pleasure in the pain of others. Got off on it. The scum of the earth.

A small croak issued from Daze's throat. "I was supposed to tell you about the pico…and get you to go to Port Station." His voice was barely audible. I leaned forward. "But I stole the quantum drive on my own. It wasn't part of the deal."

I blew out a long breath, my eyes tracking to the dark, swirling clouds above.

The kid had hedged his bets. And it'd saved his life.

Chapter 26

I met Tandor's stare with a mirthful look of my own. It had the desired effect. Tandor's face, exposed by his open, visor-less helmet, turned a ruddy red and became pinched and full of tics. "You think this is funny?" He punctuated his words with the barrel of his gun against Bender's neck, causing my friend's body to sway with each ram.

"Yes and no," I said evenly. He seemed confused, his gaze darting around. So, I explained. "The kid had already stolen from you once, which got him into this mess in the first place. Because of that, you were able to coerce him into helping you lure me in. But he was smart enough to know he was going to die once this whole game was over. So he took the quantum drive to protect his interests. Seems pretty brilliant to me." This time, I did cross my arms. "Because of that, you were forced to keep him alive until you recovered me and your precious key." My eyes met Daze's, making sure he understood the stakes. "And now that you have me, he dies."

The kid bowed his head as his body shook.

"What does that have to do with anything?" Tandor bellowed. "The bastard stole from me. He gave you something of mine, and I want it back. Give it to me, or all your friends die."

I sighed. "Everyone's going to die anyway. Do you really think we're all that naive? You came here to kill me and my friends because you don't want us interfering with your plans. In fact, you would've killed them on sight, except Daze kept us all alive by giving me the quantum drive." I knew Bender and Lockland were listening carefully to everything I said. "Whatever's on there must be pretty important. I'm assuming it's not just child-slavery records. Does it contain illegal sex stuff? That's always embarrassing."

Tandor thrummed with anger, his hands shook, making the gun wobble on Bender's neck. "What's on there is too sophisticated for your brain to comprehend." He made a move to grab Bender.

"Stop!" My voice was shrill, the threat clear. "If you kill any of my friends, including the boy, you will never get the quantum drive back. Ever. So if it's as important as you say it is, I suggest you back the fuck off."

Tandor froze. This man was used to getting what he wanted, that much was abundantly clear. He seemed to recover a little, a smug smile forming on his lips. "We'll kill you all and find it anyway."

"You can try," I agreed. "But the city is big and dirty with lots of nooks and crannies. Did Daze tell you I'm a salvager? You probably knew that already. Your drive could be literally anywhere, and when I say anywhere, you might want to start by combing the entire dead forest and look behind every tree on your way back into town."

"I'll inject you with Babble."

"You ran out." His face showed his surprise before he could mask it with a furious expression. "I mic'd you earlier." I shrugged. "Such an easy thing to do, and it garners such great results." As I talked, I constantly evaluated the situation, continuing to search for that one small opening that was going to turn this thing around. "Here's what we're going to do. You're going to let me and my friends go free, and after we're all safely tucked in, I'll arrange a place for you to pick up the quantum drive." It was an empty option. We both knew either Tandor and his men killed us, or we killed them. But stalling was never in vain. What I needed was time. "Then we all get what we want," I finished pleasantly.

Cold fury blazed off him. This man had a gigantic problem with control. I guess that's why he was a zealot and not a techie. "That isn't going to happen."

Next to him, Daze struggled to stand. Blood dripped down his face as his thin voice rang out, "I can deliver it. I know where it is."

No, no, no, kid. That's not how this is supposed to go.

"No, you don't," I challenged. "I moved it—"

Tandor interrupted me, scenting weakness. He stared at Daze with the kind of greed only a man who was confident of his own power could achieve. "Where is it?"

"I'm not telling you until you let them go." Daze had the audacity to cross his arms and jut out his chin.

Not even a second of time elapsed before Tandor's arm swung out, knocking the kid to the ground so hard his head bounced off the rocks like it was made of elastomer. "Tell me right now, or I kill the girl," he demanded, moving to stand over him. "You already lied. You told me you didn't know where it was!" So Daze had led him down a slippery path of half-truths. "I will not stand for another one of your made-up stories."

I refrained from doing a number of things, most of them having to do with bringing harm to the madman in front of me. The best thing about this scenario was that Tandor had moved away from Bender. Not far enough, his gun was still within reach of Bender's neck, but it was a start.

My heart gave an irregular beat as I watched this asshole torment Daze.

There was no other choice but to stand still and let it happen. A premature move would get me and my pals killed. I cleared my throat. "If you kill me, you don't actually get the quantum drive, since I moved it to a new location, one the kid knows nothing about." Diverting the focus away from Daze was my top priority. "I'm questioning your intelligence at this point, that you'd take a kid's word over mine, but now's the time to prove me wrong."

Tandor glared at me. "You moved it." His voice was a direct challenge.

"I already said I did."

Jamming the barrel back on Bender's neck, Tandor bent down and grabbed Daze by the leg, toppling him over, dragging him toward the edge. "Then it won't matter to you if I kill him or not." He shook Daze, making his small body bounce around. "Since he doesn't have the information I need, he doesn't need to keep breathing."

He was testing me. He didn't know which lie to believe. "That's correct—"

Daze lifted his face, blood streaming from multiple abrasions. The kid didn't have very many lives left. "She didn't move it," he sputtered weakly. "I know."

Daze was trying to protect me on his last few breaths. My heart skipped its regularly programmed beat.

"How could you possibly know that?" I challenged, shifting to my don't-take-any-shit-from-anyone face. This kid needed to stay quiet. "We've been separated for a while now. How dumb do you think I am? Do you honestly think I'd keep it where you saw me put it after I discovered that you're a two-faced liar who set me up to be killed after I took you in?"

"I know, because—"

"You know *nothing.*" I cut him off before he betrayed too much. It was clear he knew I hadn't been able to get back to Luce after the debacle in Port Station. I'd emphasized the word *nothing*, hoping to get through his thick, bruised skull.

"Stand up," Tandor demanded of Daze, dropping his leg. The zealot met my gaze gleefully, an evil look flittering over his below-average features. "I think he's telling the truth. He knows where it is."

Before I could respond, Daze agreed as he stumbled to his feet. "I do. Let them go, and I'll get it back for you."

Um, that wasn't going to happen.

I needed a fucking distraction, like yesterday.

One would do the trick.

Lockland was still on his knees just to my left. He moved his hand ever so slightly. I saw it. He was waiting, just as I was, for that single thing that would give us the opportunity to finish this.

Tandor turned toward Bender, who was so precariously close to tumbling back over the cliff, I held my breath. "None of you are necessary now."

I was just about to shout my argument about why we were so, so necessary when I heard a noise.

Props.

A craft was entering the area.

One of Tandor's men called out, "That could be Martin. He hasn't come back yet."

I didn't care who the fuck it was—it was our diversion.

As loudly as I could, I yelled, "I need a nap!"

"What?" Tandor said, his eyes distracted, pinned

over my right shoulder. They began to widen in surprise, causing me to dart a glance in that direction.

The craft was coming in much too fast.

Approximately two seconds later, everyone realized the same thing, and there was widespread panic.

Perfect. "I said I need a nap, motherfucker." Utilizing the moment, I angled my toe under the handle of my gun and lofted it into the air, catching it like I had since I was twelve. "NOW!"

Bender and Lockland reacted instantaneously.

Nap was code for *wait for my mark.*

Lockland lobbed the hydro-bomb at the men closing in behind us, while Bender plowed a shoulder into Tandor, using his considerable strength to rock him off balance.

Tandor's gun dropped off his neck just far enough.

"Down!" I screamed at both Bender and Daze as I fired my Gem, hitting Tandor squarely in the chest, the force sending him sailing off the cliff with a gaping hole running through his middle.

Bender was already rolling away from the edge, toward safety. He'd be up and ready to fight before my finger was off the trigger.

However, Daze's body began to crumple before my eyes, shock settling in. I rushed toward him, my mind screaming. He was much too close to the edge.

Everything seemed to happen in slow motion, even though I knew that wasn't the reality of the situation. Behind me, the craft was on top of us, and people were screaming. I didn't turn around.

My eyes were pinned on Daze.

The kid had been forced to trick me, but he'd made sure he'd had insurance. In the end, he'd been willing to forfeit his own life to protect us, which was the very foundation that trust was built on.

His eyes rolled back in his head as I ran. His face was a mass of blood, scratches, and bruises. He was gaunt, his coloring stark and pale underneath all the scarlet. The momentum of the fall was going to take him over the side before I could reach him. I watched in horror as his legs went first, gravity tugging at them like the bitch it was.

I was so close, but I couldn't dive for him.

My vest was full of bombs that could blow the gorge apart. "Stay with me!" I yelled as I went down on my side, for the second time, catching his thin excuse for an arm right as his body dumped over the edge.

I twisted as I moved, hauling him up and over me, as I continued my momentum. His body rolled toward safety, and I exhaled.

The view from this close to the edge sucked. The water raged hungrily below, hoping I'd fall so it could consume me. I blindly lifted my arm up, hoping someone was there. If I fell, at least the kid was safe.

Maybe in the afterlife I'd get a halo.

A large hand clasped my forearm, stabilizing me in an instant, spinning me around like I was nothing more than a doll. "Freedom's this way, dummy." The voice was gruff and familiar. "I didn't think you had a death wish."

I heaved for oxygen, my hands splayed in front of me, my head bowed, my heart racing a million kilometers an hour, my vision blurred from all the action. I drew up on my knees and brought my gloved hands to my face, taking in a few more deep breaths. Once I was collected enough, I titled my head up. "Fuck you, Bender. Can't you see I'm having a rough day?"

Chapter 27

I picked Daze up, cradling him in my arms. He couldn't have weighed more than thirty kilos at most. His body was limp. I had no idea the extent of his injuries, or if he would even make it through the night.

All I cared about was getting him to safety.

The carnage in front of me was vast. Seven sat three meters away, idling. There was blood, and limbs, and other unnamable things scattered around that I didn't want to think about. I was hardcore, but even I had limits.

Lockland and Bender stood off to the side with their arms crossed, surveying the scene. Lockland turned as I came forward. His head bobbed toward the matte black craft. "He used his props to take out the ones who stuck around. I've never seen that before, but it got the job done."

"It was gruesome as hell," Bender grunted. "But effective."

I nodded, making my way toward the craft. I popped open the pilot's-side door, still holding Daze, to find Case hunched over the controls, barely awake, his eyes struggling to stay open.

"Crawl into the passenger side," I directed as I made my way around. I unlatched the door, letting it ease open on its own, and waited for Case to untangle himself and dump himself into the passenger seat. His movements were sluggish, but he got the job done. When he was mostly upright, I settled Daze on his lap. "Make sure you cradle his head. Does your bunker have more medi supplies than the ones in that box?" It was either the barracks or Bender's place, which had some supplies, but not a great variety.

He nodded.

That was good enough for me.

I shut the door. Lockland and Bender were waiting on the other side. "Give me a day to try and save the kid," I told them. "I have a pack and a duffel, along with a hydro-launcher and extra bombs that way." I gestured into the woods as I pulled myself into the craft.

Lockland's face was grim. "They knew where we were. They picked us up a few hours in."

"I know." I placed my hands around the controls, spinning up the fans, causing the craft to bounce. "It's my fault. I'll fill you in on everything. Just give me twenty-four hours with the kid."

Bender's face was dead serious. "Can we trust him?"

I turned to Case, whose head was tilted back on the

seat, his eyes closed, his arms locked tightly around Daze. "For now." I couldn't discount that he'd arrived, barely conscious, and took out the opposition. If he hadn't, it was hard to know which way this would've gone.

Lockland patted the side of the craft and took a step back. "I hope the kid makes it."

I nodded. "Me, too."

"He put his neck on the line," Bender added. "That little shit has guts."

"He does," I agreed. I was relieved to find out that my first assessment of the kid hadn't been too far off, and my gut had been right the first time. Guts were good compasses in this crazy world. It made me happy I could still trust mine. "I dumped my tech phones a couple kilometers back so they didn't go off. I'll pick them up later. When you pick up the duffels, check the ground. I emptied my pockets. I'll meet you both at Bender's tomorrow." I reached my hand up to lower the door.

Before it closed, Lockland asked, "Do you really have the quantum drive?"

"I do if Luce is still in one piece."

Lockland's eyes brightened. "We're going to have to get hold of a pico to read it, but whatever's on there must be important if this guy and his crew were ready to die for it."

"He said it was a key," Bender added. "Whatever the fuck that means. But for us, it means we own it and need to figure it out."

"We will," I said. "We can worry about that later. After we get Darby sprung."

They both nodded as I closed the door.

I took off, gaining altitude immediately, pushing Seven to her limits. I could find my way back to the bunker on my own. As I flew, Case was in and out of consciousness. If I had to, I would wake him up.

I skirted the city, opting to head straight east to the sea.

The wind was in full force, but I barely noticed. The ocean roiled to my left as I positioned Seven to hug the coast. Daze hadn't stirred. If he had more than surface abrasions and minor cuts, there was nothing I could do. I wasn't a medic.

We could try to shuttle him to the government facility, but with the time it would take, it would likely prove fatal. The Medi Center was always crowded and was first-come, first-served, no matter how grave the injury. Sometimes you had to wait for days. They had a few medi-pods and a few "doctors" who could perform complicated surgeries, but there were too few for the masses.

As the craft moved closer to the bunker, I recognized the topography of the beach. Being good at directions was a must for a salvager. If you couldn't remember your previous location, you never made it back to claim your prize. My talent was remembering landmarks, and the large sand dune coming up in front of me was the signal to turn left out over the waves.

I swallowed any trepidation I had as I redirected Seven over the tidal currents, the thunderous crashing oddly comforting this time, probably because I knew a safe haven was close by. The sea, in all its anger, meant I was that much closer to possibly saving this kid's life.

The sky was brighter than it had been that first night, making navigation a hell of a lot easier. The craft lofted and bobbed, the turbulent air making it unstable, but I made it into the parking spot with room to spare, hitting the landing gear at the same time I popped my door. I leaned over and punched Case's arm. "Wake up. We need to get the kid inside."

I hopped out and made my way around. Case managed to spring his door, and I carefully lifted Daze from his lap. "You have to open the barricade quickly," I instructed, bending my head over the kid's chest, relieved to hear a shallow heartbeat, stepping back as Case stumbled out.

His legs were unsteady, but he stayed upright. He didn't comment as he made his way to the door. Once he was in front, he waved his hand, indicating that I should stay back. "It's rigged," he slurred. "If I mess it up, it'll blow."

No surprise there.

"Here, take the kid and let me do it." I held Daze out to him. When he seemed unsure and more than a bit confused, his brow furrowed like he was trying to figure out the very meaning of our existence on this wretched planet, I said, firmer this time, "It's either I do it, or we all die. You're in no shape to do anything more complicated than walk, and I'm sick of being on the edge of sudden death." Literally physically ill, as in my stomach had been tied in knots for hours. When he still didn't react, I reasoned, "Case, can't you just change the code later, after I leave?" He shook his head, trying to find words, but they weren't coming quickly enough. "Okay, fine, I'll make a deal with you. You tell me the code, and before I leave, I'll teach you how to rig a bomb that's undetectable under every light spectrum. Even better, I'll supply you with the materials, and you can run it wherever you want inside this parking ramp to protect your safe place. It'll be foolproof as long as you're not on the effects of a tranq dart when you get home." He stood there, his face slack. "Case! The kid will die right here if we don't get the fuck inside."

His eyes pierced mine. They were clouded, but I watched as something penetrated the confusion. He held out his arms, and I slid the kid carefully in them, squeezing by to stand in front of the door.

"What's the sequence?"

He tilted his head back. When it finally came forward, he blinked hard twice. "Two full spins to the right"—another blink—"one to the left, then back right a quarter spin"—two more blinks—"then left a half."

I examined the wheel with four spokes. One of the spokes was darker than the rest. "Is the dark mark the starting point of the turn? And does it align up or down?" I was familiar with old-fashioned bank safes, as many people before the dark days had used them, leery of having everything in their home fully computerized due to a rash of high-end tech robberies twenty years before the meteor hit. I'd salvaged a few. Didn't do much but use them for storage, as many were bomb-proof, made of half-meter-thick diamond-fiber composite. I understood the mechanisms.

"At the top."

"Excuse me?"

"Align the dark spoke up."

I held my breath and did as he instructed. Then I turned the wheel two full turns right, then one left, then right a quarter, making sure my eyes never left the mark on the wheel, then a half.

The door opened.

Case shuffled forward, handing Daze to me. He braced his shoulder against the wall, struggling to displace the thick door even a few centimeters in his sorry state. After much grunting and groaning, he finally won the battle and moved it just enough for us to slip through. I used my chin to jab on my shoulder light so we could see.

I was down the stairs and to the next door before Case closed the main one.

Once inside the cavernous room, I hit the lights with my elbow.

Laying Daze carefully on the cushioned seating, I raced over to the area where I'd seen Case get the medi supplies. I rummaged through the cupboard, removing the box he'd used, glancing inside. It wouldn't be enough. I counted five or six medi-towels, a few numbing agents, and a single narco dart. "Fuck." I set the box down and continued my frantic search of more cupboards. They were mostly empty. I turned around in frustration as Case shuffled in. "Where are all the supplies? You said this place had them!"

He motioned toward the back of the room. "There's a medi-pod back there. In the corner."

"What?" I rushed forward, refraining from grabbing him by the front of the jacket with both fists. "An actual *working* medi-pod?"

He leaned over to pick up Daze, but I shouldered him out of the way, which was easy to do since he was so unstable. "It works," he slurred, trailing after me as I raced Daze back there, scanning the area for a medi-pod I didn't see. They were usually tall, white, and cylindrical, spanning from floor to ceiling. There wasn't one in sight.

"Where is it?" Frustration leaked out all over.

"It's integrated into the wall. To your left."

Tricky.

I finally spotted a handle sticking out behind some crates. It was labeled with a red cross, the universal sign for medical aid. "Hurry up, move those pallets," I urged. Case complied. Thank goodness they were light and simple to relocate.

Some medi-pods only diagnosed, others healed minor injuries, some were hospital grade and could 3-D-print an organ for you, but unfortunately the tech to operate those had gone with the meteor.

I couldn't imagine this one would heal the kid, but at least we'd know what the damage was.

Case managed to heft the crates out of the way and drag the pod out of the wall. After the initial pull, it slid smoothly on rollers. It was horizontal, not vertical, and it was adult-sized. He hit the power button on top, and the lid opened slowly on automated brackets. Once it was fully sprung, the thing lit up like an illegal residence during blackout. Multicolored lights blinked on an intricate system board, running along the lip, the inside a pulsing neon purple.

I carefully set Daze inside. "Please be okay," I whispered as Case closed the top and pressed a green button on the side with the word *Diagnosis* on it.

The thing began to whirl like a turbine engine.

There was an orange button next to the green one that read *Heal*, which gave me a few warm fuzzies. If this was a military-grade pod, it had the potential to be more advanced than your average run-of-the-mill home units.

I refused to get my hopes up, instructing my sane brain to get back in charge of things before I crashed and burned. When expectations were elevated, it almost always went the other way. "How long does it run for?" I asked Case, only to find him walking away. "Hey," I called. He stopped and turned. I suddenly felt a little ungrateful. "Um, thank you. If you hadn't made it to the clearing when you did, we might not be here. And also for allowing me to bring Daze here. It's appreciated."

He nodded, then continued to make his way to the seating, where he collapsed.

I found a chair and dragged it next to the pod. I had no idea how long it would take to diagnose, but I figured it would stop making noise when it was done.

My eyelids drooped instantly.

Despite the adrenaline buzzing through my system, my body had had it. I crossed my arms and tried to get comfortable. It was going to be a long night and fatigue was settling in, as it did regularly after a big, exhausting event. In this world, you took rest when and where you could get it.

A loud beep sounded, and I shot off my chair like a gun had gone off next to my ear, stumbling forward. I had no idea how long I'd been asleep as I leaned over the pod, wiping the crust from my eyes, searching for a readout of some kind.

The sound of Case's voice so close surprised me. "This pod can only fix minor ailments." He was almost to us, his gait steady, his eyes alert.

"How long have we been out?" I asked, blinking myself awake.

"It's been about two and a half hours."

That seemed like a long time for diagnosis. I scanned the top of the pod, but couldn't find any words, only blinking lights. "How do you read this thing?"

"The screen is on the inside." He stood next to me and opened the lid.

Daze looked so small lying inside.

His face was still covered in dried blood, but his chest was moving up and down at regular intervals. That was a good sign. "What does it say?"

Case read the digital scanner, which scrolled by at a quick clip. "Three broken bones. A rib, the hamate bone in his left hand, and a hairline fracture in his ulna. Some of his organs are bruised, but not bleeding. He has fifteen cuts to his outer epidermis—I think that's his skin—and a 'maxi' concussion, which I assume is worse than a mini."

"Okay." I glanced down, mildly surprised to find my hands clasped in front of my body like I was trying to make a wish. "That all sounds healable."

Case leaned forward as the digital screen morphed, flashing new text. "He's also severely dehydrated, malnourished, and his vitamin D levels are below acceptable levels." Case glanced at me, his face grim. "Without intervention, it says he will die within twenty-four hours."

My hands shot apart as I raked them through my hair, turning in a circle. "What are we supposed to do? How do we help him?"

Case depressed a small button next to the screen, and it flickered. He read the new text out loud. "First, he needs water. Then we need to clean his outer wounds, place him back in, and press the *Heal* button." He stepped away, shrugging. "That's all it says."

"You get the water, and I'll swab him with some medi-towels."

Forcing water down an uncooperative throat was harder than it sounded. Or maybe it was as hard as it sounded. Daze didn't wake up, but he did sputter and cough. I made him drink three glasses. One was aminos to give him some extra nutrients.

Next, I ran medi-towels over him and watched in fascination as some of the minor wounds closed instantly. I also decided to give him a numbing dart to help with the pain when he woke up.

Once we were done, I closed the lid and pressed *Heal*.

Now we waited.

I made a move to sit back down in the chair, and Case said, "Go get some rest in a sleeping pod. I'll stay here."

"No, thanks. I got it." I took my seat.

Instead of arguing, Case got his own chair. "It could take hours."

"I'm sure it will." We sat in silence, the whirl of the machine calmer this time. Apparently, healing was less forceful than diagnosing. After about fifteen minutes of silence, I said, "I don't think your sister made it out alive, but I can't be sure. I didn't get a good look at everyone. But she was there. I heard her talk about you."

"She wasn't my birth sister. And that's perfectly fine. It means I don't have to go find her and do it myself."

I peered at him, my arms crossed, trying to relax as much as I could in a straight-backed chair, my back and neck already cricked from sleeping in this position for over two hours. "You made a deal with Tandor to rat me out, but not to protect your sister—to *kill* her?"

He didn't answer immediately.

After a while, he finally murmured, "We'd been together since our time on the streets and then eventually were sustained by the same family. She was vile, one of those people who never thought before she acted. She valued her own pleasure over others. She had a child ten years ago. Her son was loving, loyal, funny, and bright."

"Frankie."

He didn't question how I knew the child's name. "She didn't deserve him. She killed him because Tandor told her to. She did it gleefully and horribly. She made him suffer. I vowed to track her down if it was the last thing I ever did, and today it seems I kept my promise."

We sat in silence again.

About an hour later, the machine stopped, alerting us with another loud beep. I stood, dropping my arms. "That's it?" A green light blinked on the top, so it must be. Case stood next to me. "Do you think he stopped breathing or something? Is that why it quit?"

"There's only one way to find out." Case opened the lid.

The kid's eyes were closed, but his coloring looked

better, healthier. The ultraviolet light must've been on continuously. "What does the readout say?"

"His bones are set. His vitamin D is now at a minimum acceptable level. Hydration is noncritical. It says he needs rest and food. Then back here for a week of daily treatments."

I grinned. "Seriously? This thing is my new best friend." I caressed the top of it in silent thanks before I lifted Daze out. As I adjusted him in my arms, his eyes opened.

"Holly?" His voice was raspy and hoarse, breaking on the last syllable of my name.

"Yeah?"

"I didn't mean to lie to you. I just didn't know what to do."

"Don't worry about it." I walked us toward the sleeping pods.

"I knew the quantum drive would save you. At least for a while. Tandor really needed it."

"That was smart. And, by the way, I forgive you."

"You do?" He tried to lean forward, but he was too weak. I reorganized him, letting his head fall against my shoulder.

"Yep. But if you ever do anything like that again, I'm not risking my life to rescue your skinny butt off that damn gorge. Twice is my limit."

His eyes closed. "Okay, deal." Half a beat later, they flew open again, his heart racing as it pattered against my arm. "Are you still going to sustain me? I can understand if you don't want to anymore—"

"Yes. I am. You're not going to get rid of me that easily. But, by my count, you owe me big-time, and I'm thinking it's going to take at least a year—maybe two—to pay me back." Daze nodded, satisfied with my answer, his eyes drifting shut once again. Case stood next to a sleeping pod, and I set Daze inside. Then I leaned over and unlaced my boots and unzipped my vest, leaving my guns where they were, strapped to my waist. I crawled in next to him, gently shifting his body to the side. There was more than enough room for the both of us. These military pods were huge. As Case began to shut the lid, I growled, "Set it for twelve hours, and I swear on the accuracy of my Gem, if you sedate me again, I will know it. I'm not averse to kicking your ass a third time."

"You're safe. At least for tonight." A tiny glimmer of a smile flirted at the ends of his lips.

It was possible Case had dimples, but I'd likely never see them again, so I wasn't going to dwell on it overmuch.

The lid went down, and I closed my eyes. Sleep sounded good. The chair had been fitful at best, and my entire body ached, the adrenaline totally gone now. In its place was cold, hard fatigue.

My mind drifted immediately to Darby. First thing tomorrow, we'd figure out a way to get him back, and life would go back to its normal, dreary self.

My eyes flicked open. I almost laughed out loud.

I was lying next to my kid. A kid I'd already disowned and then reowned in the span of two days.

Things were never going to be normal again. The best I could hope for was something new.

The lid of the sleeping pod next to me shut.

A new normal.

I'm sure it would be as easy as one, two, three.

DANGER'S VICE

A HOLLY DANGER NOVEL: BOOK TWO

AMANDA CARLSON

Chapter 1

"What do you mean she's in holding?" I paced in front of the worktable where Lockland sat, fingers pressed to his temples like he was trying to push back a headache. That made two of us. "What the hell is *holding*, anyway?" I braced my fists on top of the cool metal, leaning over so I could get my answer up close and personal.

I was tired. Sleep had been evasive at best. Daze had almost died the night before, so I'd been up on and off, never really settling into any good REM.

But the kid was better, so that was a plus.

I'd arrived in Port Station this morning to pick up my craft, only to find her missing. She'd been parked in a hard-to-reach location—like on-top-of-a-building hard to reach.

"I'm working on it." Lockland raised his head. Smudges darkened the skin underneath his eyes, indicating he hadn't slept all that well either. "The guards brought Luce in."

The table in Bender's workshop that I was hovering over was covered in junk. Pixie motors, dirty rags, random fittings, and for the first time I noticed some distinctly shaped items of the personal pleasure variety.

I stood, raising a single eyebrow.

Doing my best to ignore the assortment of colorful and unnaturally glossy toys, I made my way over to a nearby chair and sat. I sighed. "Where did they take her, exactly?" I tried to brush my hair away from my face, but my fingers got hooked in the uncooperative mess. It fell around my shoulders in thick, ropy strands, saturated with sweat and who knew what else. A trip to a cleaning stall was high on my to-do list. After everything else. "And how did they achieve that? She was on top of a fucking building. At an angle."

"They have a mover drone," Lockland replied. Along with the half moons shadowing his lower lids, the jet-black stubble tracing his currently clenched jaw was longer than usual, and his short hair was in need of a trim. Seeing Lockland unkempt was strange, as the man took it to heart to stay kempt, but I understood why. None of us had had time to do anything other than survive the last few days. "Like people used before the dark days, to transport large objects like floating craft and construction bots."

"Yeah, I know what a mover drone is. Thanks for that." I stood, frustrated that we'd found ourselves in this predicament. It'd been a lot of years since anyone had gotten the best of us. We were a solid team, working as a unit to help each other stay alive. It was the only way to survive in this city. We all had a talent. Mine was salvaging and positioning my ear to the ground, making sure nobody messed with us, and if they did, they paid for it.

I'd failed big-time and missed something huge.

Outskirts had descended into town two months prior, with plans to take over the city. It was unacceptable. The only saving grace was that I'd made their leader pay by shooting a big hole through his chest, almost losing my life in the process. I had zero regrets. I'd do it again in a heartbeat.

I wandered toward the large graphene wall that separated us from the outside, my boots clacking over the chipped mezzanine floor. Bender's shop was enormous. It used to house retail space before disaster struck, back when industry had thrived. Instead of like now, when making do by salvaging and repairing whatever the hell you could find was all we had.

Resting a shoulder against one of the pillars, I crossed my arms. "There's something extremely valuable stored inside Luce"—my head bobbed toward Lockland, and then Bender, who sat on his usual stool, stationed close to the cooling unit—"and it's imperative we get her back as soon as possible."

The quantum drive that Daze, my new sustainee, had stolen from Tandor, the zealot freak who'd threatened to take over the government, was tucked away inside a secret compartment under Luce's dash. We had no idea what was on it, but whatever data it contained—it was important. The odds that the guards in Port Station had discovered it were iffy, but they existed. My hidey-holes did their jobs well.

"We'll get her back," Bender said gruffly as he stood.

"I sure as hell hope so," I commented. "Any word on Darby's location?" Our friend and resident tech wizard-slash-scientist had been detained by the government. We'd had very little news thus far.

"No," Lockland answered. "Claire has been unresponsive."

"Since when?" I dropped my arms, my burgeoning headache forgotten in an instant.

"Late last night."

Bender grabbed a large box off a shelf and brought it over to a worktable where he began rummaging inside for something, his large biceps straining as he moved. Bender was one of the most intimidating presences in the dark city. His shiny, bald dome gleamed without a speck of hair and his muscles were corded with stark definition. He stood a head taller than most, and used the height to his advantage. "That's not like her," he grumbled, his face aimed inside the box, his hands moving things around. "Something has to be wrong."

"I couldn't agree more," I said, watching what he was doing. "She always picks up." I addressed Lockland, "What did she say when you last spoke with her?"

"The conversation was a little strange," Lockland admitted, joining us. "She sounded distant and hurried."

"Distant how?" I plucked up the object Bender had just set on the table and turned it over in my hand. It resembled a hydro-bomb, but it had a hard, bumpy coating. "You were conversing on a tech phone. How could she sound distant?" I glanced at Bender. "What the hell are these things?" It sat heavy in my palm. Bombs were light, usually made of compressed, highly flammable air.

Bender grinned. "It's a fuel rocket. I remembered I had these once we came back from dealing with that asshole, Tandor. They would've come in handy."

I examined the new toy. "These are totally back-in-the-day bombs, but they give a nice directional blast, from what I've heard. I've never used one." The top of the oval was less dense than the rest of the body. It was meant to break first, localizing the explosion. I met Lockland's gaze across the table. His mouth turned down in a frown as I continued to manhandle the object. "What? These things have a tough skin and the activate switch is tucked inside a false bottom." I slid my thumb over the rough exterior to prove my point. "It's not going to break in my hand." He said nothing, but his eyes continued to judge the situation like a father would a child's naughty behavior. I set the blaster down carefully and huffed, crossing my arms. "Fine. You haven't finished telling us why Claire sounded distant. Please continue…"

DANGER'S VICE is available now! Don't miss out on the further adventures of Holly & her crew.

NOTHING IS CREATED WITHOUT A GREAT TEAM.

My thanks to:

Awesome Cover design: Damonza

Digital and print formatting: Author E.M.S

Copyedits/proofs: Joyce Lamb

Final proof: Marlene Engel

ABOUT THE AUTHOR

Amanda Carlson is a graduate of the University of Minnesota, with a BA in both Speech and Hearing Science & Child Development. She went on to get an A.A.S. in Sign Language Interpreting and worked as an interpreter until her first child was born. She's the author of the high octane Jessica McClain urban fantasy series published by Orbit, the Sin City Collectors paranormal romance series, the contemporary fantasy Phoebe Meadows series, and the futuristic/dystopian Holly Danger series. Look for these books in stores everywhere. She lives in Minneapolis with her husband and three kids.

Find her all over social media

Website: amandacarlson.com
Facebook: facebook.com/authoramandacarlson
Twitter: @amandaccarlson
Instagram: @author_amanda

www.ingramcontent.com/pod-product-compliance
Lightning Source LLC
Chambersburg PA
CBHW050802190726
48285CB00005B/1755